IN THE KINGDOM OF CHEESE THERE ARE NO HEROES

LESLEY CHOYCE

Cover design: Rebekah Wetmore
Editor: Andrew Wetmore
ISBN: 978-1-998149-69-8
First edition February 2025

Moose House Publications
2475 Perotte Road, Annapolis County, NS B0S 1A0
moosehousepress.com
info@moosehousepress.com

Moose House Publications recognizes the support of the Province of Nova Scotia. We are pleased to work in partnership with the Department of Communities, Culture and Heritage to develop and promote our cultural resources for all Nova Scotians.

We live and work in Mi'kma'ki, the ancestral and unceded territory of the Mi'kmaw People. This territory is covered by the "Treaties of Peace and Friendship" which Mi'kmaw and Wolastoqiyik (Maliseet) People first signed with the British Crown in 1725. The treaties did not deal with surrender of lands and resources but in fact recognized Mi'kmaq and Wolastoqiyik (Maliseet) title and established the rules for what was to be an ongoing relationship between nations. We are all Treaty people.

Also by Lesley Choyce

...continued next page

Last Chance
Living Outside the Lines
Los Pandemonium
Magnificent Obsessions
The Man Who Borrowed the Bay of Fundy
Margin of Error
Never the Same Sea Twice
Nova Scotia: Shaped By the Sea
Off the Grid
Peggy's Cove: the Amazing History of a Coastal Village
Plank's Law
Random
Raising Orion
Rat
Reaction
Reckless
Refuge Cove
Re-Inventing the Wheel
The Republic of Nothing
Revenge of the Optimist
Rock
Roid Rage
The Rules Have Changed
Running the Risk
Saltwater Chronicles
Scam
Sea of Tranquility
The Second Season of Jonas MacPherson
Seven Ravens
Shoulder the Sky
Sid the Kid and the Dryer
Skateboard Shakedown
Skate Freak
Skatefreaks Og Graesrodder
Skunks for Breakfast
Smoke and Mirrors
Some Kind of Hero
Sudden Impact
The Ledge
The Summer of Apartment X
The Thing You're Good At
The Top of the Heart
The Unlikely Redemption of John Alexander MacNeil
The Untimely Resurrection of John Alexander MacNeil
Thin Places
Transcendental Anarchy
The Trap Door To Heaven
Thunderbowl
Typographical Eras
Wave Warrior
Wavewatch
World Enough
Wrong Time, Wrong Place

In memory of Doug Barron,
a great creative friend and fellow SurfPoet

This is a work of fiction. The author has created the characters, conversations, interactions, and events; and any resemblance of any character to any real person is coincidental.

In The Kingdom of Cheese
There Are No Heroes

8

Chapter One

In The Kingdom of (grilled) Cheese Sandwiches, there are no heroes. Not back then, anyway. That's what I used to say.

But maybe there were some. Maybe I was wrong.

I, for one, could have been my own hero if I was willing to break out of my shell. Break out of myself. Break out of my body.

Which shapes which? I have to ask you. Does the body shape the mind or the mind the body?

In my case, it's probably a chicken and egg situation. Chicken kingdoms and egg kingdoms also exist in my world, on my planet.

Which planet is it? you might ask. Have you not guessed?

Planet Large, some would say. Or Grand. Call me plus-size. *Beaucoup du big.* I don't know.

When people see me, they always see the oversized body I am in. No one would guess I was once a skinny little runt. A snot-nosed, snivelling little fart of a boy running down the street just for the sheer reckless joy of running down the street.

I can still see myself running. Just running and running. Like the wind. Like the antelope. Like the deer. There was a bicycle for speed and a skateboard for daring and for cool.

And a Tarzan rope swing for arcing out over the dirty, scum-covered pond and releasing me to splash down in the dark, dangerous waters.

In my mind, I still go back to those early days. Pre-twelve, pre-Twinkie, pre-KFC, pre-pudding, pre-Mars bars, pre-pretzel fest, pre-(um) *large*.

I did a lot of eating before I was twelve years old and I was as normal as normal could be. But then eating became big in my life and I *became* big.

I grew and grew. From eight to twelve I had a growth spurt. The bones in my arms and legs extended themselves of their own accord. And I ate like a horse then. But when my bones stopped ratcheting outward, there at the pivotal age of twelve years young, my body went horizontal instead of vertical. I became vertically challenged and horizontally enhanced.

Not the first boy on the block to encounter that, you might say. But skinny little me got lost in the evolution. Don't know how it happened.

Well, yes, I do. Sort of.

Old Doc Smythe weighed me at the end of my twelfth year on the planet (which is really the day you turn twelve, not the end of it) and he scratched his head and rechecked the scale. "Holy Moly, Mother of God," he said, in a most un-professional manner. "Where did little Johnny go?"

Little Johnny was that kid on the skateboard he'd once seen racing hell-bent down the steep curves of Delano Drive. Little Johnny was me—John Francis Cummings.

JFC they call me now. Like KFC without the chicken.

Where *did* little Johnny go?

Nowhere, really. He is there inside the larger boy. Screaming to get out. Trying to adjust to his new skin, his new volume, his new identity in which everyone—nearly abso-fucking-lutely everyone—sees him as the big boy on the street, in the class, on the bus, and at the window table down at Mickey D's, eating whatever large size new thing is on the menu.

Because the eyes are so often on me and the skinny masses of humanity are, in their minds if not on their tongues, labelling me, the skinny kid wants to scream. Well, so does this other kid that is also me.

Has it been yet established that a young man like me, now sixteen years from heaven, as the poet once said, is more than the sum of his body weight? If it has not, I would assert that he is.

Dreams and visions, daydreams and nightmares, daily hopes and hindrances. I am, alas, a fully human being. Do not shed a tear for me, Argentina, but please also do not ask me to shed my weight.

I am who I am because that is who I am.

And so, in the Kingdom of (grilled) Cheese Sandwiches, I must, I reassert, I *must* be my own human hero.

Long live JFC. Long live the adventures of the knight of the round, full table. To cheese or not to cheese, that is the question.

Chapter Two

I once actually wrote an essay about the history of cheese. I didn't realize I'd have to read it out loud in class.

Mr. Drummond said it was one of the best essays a sixth grader had ever written. And I bet it was. English was one of my better subjects.

Now, an oversized boy in sixth grade standing in front of the class reading an essay about the history of cheese is not what you normally see in school. And it was inevitable that there would be giggling and funny looks and every attempt by young louts to humiliate the formidable lad. That's why it was such a great test of my ability-to-keep-my-cool skills taught to me by my next-door neighbour, Mr. Jackson.

He seemed quite old at the time. I think he was sixty, but now he's even older. And I'm sixteen myself, which also would have seemed old to me back when I was in sixth grade. He still counsels me about important things sometimes, so I will tell you more about Mr. J later; but for now, all you need to know is that Mr. J has always spoken to me in short sentences that he believes are filled with wisdom.

For example, I was sitting on his porch one afternoon, watching the cars go by, and he said, "Water flows downhill. Always remember that."

And, as you can see, I have.

But that very same day, he said, "You're here for a good time, not a long time."

Later that day, when he felt a bit more talkative, he said that he had borrowed both items of wisdom. The water line came from an ancient Chinese book called *The Art of War* (which is not necessarily about war, he said). And the time line came from an old pop song that was stuck in his head.

I took both bits of borrowed wisdom to heart.

But the most important thing he told me back then, the thing that saved me over and over, the thing that saved me from humiliation the day of the out-loud cheese essay reading, was this: "No one can really get to you. Only *you* can get to you."

There were other teachings that enhanced that point, many of them borrowed from Zen Buddhism. Mr. Jackson was a Zen Buddhist. Or at least he said he was. He was also a retired nuclear physicist. Or at least he said he was.

Anyway, I believed him. He was my friend. Still is, really. And ally. Guru, Zen master, next door neighbour. A guy who admitted he wasted much of his life trying to improve the overall function of an explosive nuclear device.

"Don't make the mistakes I did," he told me. So I've ruled out nuclear physics and weapon design as career options.

There's probably not much more to tell about the essay reading. Except that no one *got* to me. Not even me. I stayed cool. I knew even then I was here for a good time, not a long time, so I didn't want to waste any of it.

Chapter Three

It's taking me a while to get to the heart of this story, as you can most likely tell. I know you probably think I'm going to start complaining about bullies.

Bullies get way too much press coverage, and even though several will appear in this tale, with one outstanding teenage example of the species, I want to say for the record that I don't personally have a problem with them. I learned to handle them early on. Maybe it was something Mr. J told me about allowing someone else's force against you to your advantage. According to him you can use everything—good or bad—to your own advantage if you know how.

Same goes for bullies.

A schoolyard bully is identifiable. You can see him, hear him, smell him and almost (yuck) taste him. He begins practising his craft from a very young age and by the time he arrives in the so-called educational system, he has become most adept at identifying his victims. Skinny whiny little me back in the early short-pants days of pedagogic servitude appeared to be a worthy (and easy) target, but I actually was not. And by the time I became the much larger insult-hurling focus of the class, I had established what I call "my cool." This is a skill you may want to cultivate on your own if you are not a citizen of cool.

Why cool?

Well, I sort of had no choice. My mother, as you see, has always been (to my knowledge) crazy.

I know we often say that about our mothers. But mine really was. She has a temper and is unable to control her emotions. So often, over the years of my evolution from small, wiry, running rascal with scraped-up knees and elbows into the teenage big boy, my mom has freaked out at home, with me as the only audience. She tries very hard to hold it together in public, but is not always successful.

"I have very legitimate reasons to be mad," she has explained to me more than a thousand times.

And indeed she does. She had a tough childhood with an abusive father. "I could sell the damn story to a producer and he could make a million dollars on it as a mini-series," she'd say. And then there is the factor of my disappearing father.

Yes, the Invisible Man, as she likes to call him. "He was invisible even when he was here," she says. But then one day he really vanished. Without a trace.

I remember him, but not well. He really was sort of invisible. He didn't have much of a personality, if I recall correctly, but he was my father, and I sort of wish I had fond memories. I don't.

I mean, I truly don't have much memory of him at all. He was quiet—quiet and troubled about something that I could never figure out. "Not quite comfortable in his own skin," was what Mr. Jackson explained in retrospect, after my father departed for unknown regions.

My mother blames *Star Wars* and has never forgiven George Lucas. And never, ever mention Luke Skywalker or Darth Vader in her presence. You see, my father, one day in that long time ago, was looking really antsy and he said he was going to go to the movies to watch the latest *Star Wars* movie (I think it was the really bad one). And he never came back.

My mother raged and threw things, her way to express anger. There was breakage and shouting and I was the appointed audience, as noted. But then she calmed down, as she so often does after a bout of rage. And I held her as she cried.

My poor mom.

I'd like to say that, deep down, she is a good mother. But that's probably an exaggeration. She is who she is. And I am her son. And this, as they say, is the hand that I've been dealt.

Which does make me wonder sometimes, who exactly is the dealer?

At least my dad wasn't a bully. He was probably more a victim. A victim of life's circumstances who had not developed proper coping mechanisms. Maybe if he had been able to express his anger like Mom, he might have stayed. Sometimes it makes me wish they had fought more.

But they didn't. And then he was gone. And all I could say to no one was, *So long, Dad. Hope you are well somewhere on the earth.*

~

So, before I completely get on with my story, let me say again that I'm strangely okay with the bullies of the world. I understand the plight of the invisible fathers and angry mothers. It's the liars and cheats who most ruffle my feathers. More on that in a minute.

I've always had a problem with the word "bully" because it's usually only used when someone is giving a lecture in print or in a speech about this type of person. Your handy thesaurus might tell you that you could replace the word with tormentor, persecutor, oppressor, tyrant or intimidator but they are all rather large words for a small story like this.

Bullies do all of those things and more, but they do it at an individual level. It's not a national thing until you have a truly psychotic leader and, in case you haven't noticed, every now and then people decide they rather love such dark stars and let them lead a nation into tormenting and oppressing other nations.

The verbs associated with such callous operators include intimidate, terrorize, persecute, torment, frighten, oppress, browbeat and harass. These, too, sound ominously loud and large, so I need to stick to the basics of my story and not get carried away with anything Mr. Roget (of thesaurus fame) can come up with.

Verbiage aside, let me give it/them/him a name: Larkin Kelsey.

I know that Larkin Kelsey sounds more like a lawyer— and perhaps he will one day be just that. A lawyer like his father. Larkin is also a liar and a cheat and that has put him on my bad list since grade one, or maybe it was grade two.

It was thanks to him, in fact, that I learned the word

"browbeat" (noted above). He had a way of wearing down his victims using this methodology until he was ready to move in for the kill.

But remember, we were only little tykes in those days. I was still the skinny rabbit of a child and could easily let the browbeating slide off me like water off a duck, to mix up my metaphors. He could muster all kinds of cruel little things to bite at me with—comments about my hair, the shape of my nose, my mother's selection of footwear, my chin, even. How can you browbeat a person over their chin, you might ask? Well, Larkin was good at even that.

Larkin had been left back a year in school when he was younger. He claimed his father forced the school to keep him back a year as punishment for bad grades. Too bad for everyone who was my age in our town. After that, we were stuck with him down through the years.

Now he had his driver's license and drove the shiny black Mustang his father bought him to school.

A long time ago I adopted a strategy to defuse the young Lark the Fark. It was called The Shrug. And, oddly enough, my father had taught it to me. My mom would light up like the Fourth of July with a string of complaints about the Invisible Father and he'd just shrug.

I tried it out on Lark as he tried to belittle me in front of my classmates with a tirade of insults about my very own mother—whom he didn't even know and had never met.

I was amazed that someone could go on so long about one's dear old mom. But Larkin would throw insults at ice cream if he wanted to. So when he started stringing together horrible words and insults about my mom (strangely, some of them were somewhat true), I imagined him harassing something we all loved deeply back then—I'm referring to ice cream, of course. And I found it funny.

Not funny enough to laugh. No, you generally don't want to laugh at your tormentor. Laughter's good medicine for many things, but it can be like gasoline tossed into a hot cast-iron pan of bacon on your stove. So best to save it for watching dumb cat videos on YouTube or wherever.

When we were just kids, The Shrug did a serviceable job of getting Larkin off my case and he would just stomp off and pick on someone else. But as we grew older I began to realize my childish defence mechanisms no longer had the same effect.

Chapter Four

By now you are wondering why no one has coached me how to get on with my story. My English teachers down through all the grades have said I have a wonderful capacity to digress. In fact, one of them, Mr. Cronkite back in seventh grade, said just that after I gave a long-winded answer in class concerning a simple little poem called "The Death of a Moth."

"John Francis, you have a wonderful capacity to digress," he said. And one of Larkin's cronies, a real tool in the toolbox of faulty pliers, said this out loud: "More like a wonderful capacity to digest." This was after I had already started to bulk up and turn the thin lad into a more significant physical person.

The class thought it was funny. Mr. C did not. But others repeated the phrase to me later that year, a strange and annoying echo of a humorous insult. It was nothing I couldn't handle.

Larkin used it himself as a kind of anthem sometimes when he saw me shuffling down the shiny hallway. Larkin, as you can probably note, was not the creative sort. He used mostly one- and two-syllable words for his insults, words that you could not get away with around most adults. He was more like the type to sneak up behind you and kick you right behind your knees, one at a time, but quickly, so that you might fold like a lawn chair right there in the school hallway.

But let us proceed to the major event and backfill the story as seems appropriate.

To set the scene, I'll take you into the locker room at our somewhat-dilapidated high school. The time is right after gym class on a Thursday.

Oh, no, you say, *not the quintessential locker room scene.*

Well, not quite, but close. These things do happen more often than you think. But hang in there. It's not all smacking boys' butts with wet towels and scathing insults about their anatomy.

We had been running around in the gym for a good hour, playing dodgeball. This vile athletic activity had been banned in many schools, but Mr. Simms, who had been around teaching since before the invention of cell phones, said he didn't give a rat's ass about what other Phys Ed teachers did. He thought dodgeball was a "tried and true" sport.

So there we were, the boys of grade eleven, throwing the dodgeball at the feet of our male classmates to knock them down so we could watch them kiss the shiny hardwood floor hard enough to split a lip or two.

Apparently, during this session of high school athletic prowess, Brady Quinn had somehow insulted Larkin Kelsey. Brady was diminutive for his age, and tried to make up for it by being a classic smart-ass who would say anything to anyone at any time if he thought he could hurt their feelings.

His parents had stamped the word "Victim" on his forehead at a very young age and he seemed to go looking to get into arguments or even to get beat up.

I'd advised him more than once to learn to tether his insulting instincts and use his clever wit for more positive things. But he usually ended up saying things about my mother or trying to explain to me why it was my fault that my father left us. (Because my mother and I, he would improvise, were "abominable losers living in Loserville, and anyone in their right mind would take the bus right out of there for good.")

Now, I could always forgive Brady for all this and would have still considered him a high school colleague, if not a friend, if he had not also been a liar and a cheat. He told everyone his family was rich, but they lived in a rundown, second-hand trailer in a mobile home park on a street named after one of the Seven Dwarves. (No, not Dopey but one of the other lesser-known ones.)

So, without further ado, let me return to the scene of the crime—my crime, as it turned out.

The said locker room smelled badly. Brady was there, having had his fill of providing snotty blow-by-blow commentary in the gym during dodgeball. Larkin, of course, was presiding over the scene. At least two of Larkin's friends were there—Harrison and Jimmy. And me, of course. There were others but you get the picture. And we are all standing around shirtless and in our underwear.

Ultimately, it was the picture that was the problem. Or a video, really. A precisely edited video that showed what I did.

And what did I do that caused such a stir? What was the thing that got me into such hot water? That convinced over half of the high-school population that, beneath my mild exterior, I was a dangerous, violent psychopath?

Well, since you asked, here is what was posted on social media and went (I hate this term) viral.

What you see is me, large around the middle, clothed only in my Walmart-brand boxer shorts, shoving none other than Larkin Kelsey face-first into the wall of lockers and holding him there with his right arm radically jerked up behind his back.

I have more weight than him, so this was not terribly difficult. My sweaty chest is up against his back and I am pushing him into the locker and butting my head against the back of his as if to punctuate the statement I am trying to make.

There is much screaming on the part of Larkin and I can feel the rage that tenses up his body as I hold him in this sumo-wrestling sort of stance for several awkward but triumphant seconds as the boys in the locker room look on with dropped jaws, rude commentary and snickering.

Harrison, of course has his phone out and, like a true accomplice to cruelty, misfortune and disaster, records everything.

There is a scene that takes place before the seemingly *teenage psycho slams school football hero into metal* event, but I will save that for the moment. (Did I mention that, despite all that you now know about Larkin Kelsey, teachers and most students like him and he is also a star athlete?)

Now, Harrison is a worthy video documentarian who has

the creative insight to capture on his phone both the before and after of the event in which JFC slams Larkin Kelsey. But he has a critical eye for editing and ultimately decides that a thirty-second version of the events will play out better on both local and global websites, so what the world sees is just what he thinks is the best part. And the best part, according to his tortured little pea-sized brain, is that he posts his masterpiece with the suggestion that, *for no reason at all*, I attacked and head-smashed Larkin Kelsey.

And so, the metaphorical shit hit the proverbial fan.

Chapter Five

You deserve to know what events led up to such a strange, bizarre and downright ugly encounter. But I'll hold off on that and simply ask you, if you saw such a thing on your newsfeed, what might you make of it?

Like the multitude of other people (local, national and global) who commented, you might think I was some kind of insane sadist—someone doing something cruel and hateful to his classmate. I mean, I saw the video, the edited thirty seconds that were posted, and it did look monstrously bad. What kind of person would do this? What kind of school are they running there? Is there no decency left in the world? Who is that horror of a human who is not behind bars?

Yes, they actually said that. *About me.* In the eyes of the world, I am now that thing, that word, that harasser of all that is good, the evil manifestation of all that is wrong with the world, etc., etc.

Might I point out that my other Phys Ed classmates, standing around dishabillé, just took in the show like dorky semi-clad teenagers. I was neither egged on nor exhorted to desist. It was just a pretty good show for an otherwise dull afternoon at the ole secondary school, until Mr. Simms heard the ruckus and scrambled into the locker room, blowing his whistle.

And that ended that.

Larkin said he would "get me back" under his breath, but everyone heard it. I kept telling myself I did what I had to do.

But when Simms asked what this was all about, neither Larkin nor I answered. You would think at least one of those present at the debacle would have said something, but no one did. Not even Brady.

And that didn't surprise me.

~

I suppose this is one of those interludes in which I feel a need to say a few more words about myself. And spill a fair bit more ink about Larkin.

So, for the record, there was nothing particularly difficult about my pinning Larkin against the locker. I would have much preferred to be fully clothed and, had I not just witnessed what I had witnessed, I would not have head-butted him into the metal locker door. Even at that, I didn't do any damage to his thick skull and his diabolical brain pan. And it was all over so quickly, once I had made my move, that I was in disbelief that it had even happened.

The pacifist in me, however, was appalled. The Zen master in my soul fled.

And then, suddenly, there were no peers left in the locker room to even criticize or congratulate me. Once Mr. Simms blew the riot whistle, my esteemed classmates dressed in a most hasty manner and flew out of the locker room.

Simms looked at Larkin and me, both of us breathing heavily. Larkin had that classic look that said he wanted to kill me.

The coach said, "I want to see you both in my office."

But Larkin threw on his pants, a solid-blue button-down shirt, a two-hundred-dollar pair of running shoes and huffed off, leaving his socks and his dignity on the locker room floor.

Simms was left looking at me. His disgust was visceral. What must he have been thinking of me?

I fumbled with my clothes and eventually stuffed my considerable girth back into pants and shirt, but my brain was abuzz with wondering what had just happened. It wasn't like me to "act out", as my mom would say. I was the silent type usually, often trying to make friends with my inner peace rather than confronting the outer world in any aggressive or strategic way.

But apparently something about me had changed.

Simms now seemed at a loss for words. He looked hard into my eyes, blew one long wail on that damn whistle and then let out a guttural sound—an "ugh" or "erhh" or something that doesn't have letters to fit it. He turned on his heel and left.

And that was that. Or was it?

Of course not. Harrison was already in the boys' washroom down the hall, posting his brief, truncated documentary that apparently the cyberworld had been waiting for for such a long time.

I was expecting Simms to call the principal and that I'd

get paged to the office to sit on a hard-backed chair and stare down the end of my high school career, listen to the death knell of any possibility of ever going to university, a dire prediction from the principal (or maybe the VP) that I was headed down a dark path that would lead to prison. Or some such thing.

But that didn't happen. Not then, anyway.

I went to history class. I started to get looks. I went inside myself and reminded the worriedest part of me that water still runs downhill. That this too shall pass. That time is not necessarily linear. And even if it is, life in the cosmic scheme of things is relatively short and I will eventually die or at least pass on to the next realm, where I won't have a large hulking body at all and where my spirit might sing or soar or something even better.

I think every kid in the class had their phone out, half hidden under their desk but still rather obvious to anyone paying attention.

Mr. Tidewell had long ago given up trying to tell his uncaring students to shut off their damn cell phones during his lectures. Today, he was expounding about English explorers in the Arctic. They were all trying, and failing, to find the ever-elusive Northwest Passage. Ships stuck in ice, shortage of supplies, lead poisoning from canned food. Several explorers returned to England and lied about finding this shortcut to China. One in particular became quite the talk of the town in London, quite the little British hero, and somehow or another he ended up being one of the first governors of North Carolina. Unfortunately, I can't remember his name.

If I learned nothing else from Mr. T it is that much of human history is shaped by men (and a few select women) who lie and cheat. The bullies are omnipresent, too, of course, but it's the liars and cheats who rule the roost—sometimes with the help of their cooperative, belligerent cohorts.

So, as the explorers froze to death or became hometown heroes with their false promises, I came to the conclusion that Mr. Simms had not reported me to the office after all. I took a deep breath and tried to achieve what Mr. Jackson called the Zen "no mind." But it wasn't easy.

The bell rang just about then, tragically reinforcing the notion that time probably is linear after all. Harrison's little changing room video was now in circulation throughout the school, if not throughout the world, and I feared that he had uploaded just the part of me, large psychoboy, doing his best to injure an important high-school athlete, including the aforementioned almost involuntary head butt.

I stayed put at my desk as my classmates filed out of the room. Each one had a look for me that stated an awful opinion about my personage. As I hoisted myself out of the chair at last, I tried to steel myself for what might be difficult days ahead.

And I was probably still trying to steel myself when Robin found me in the hall. She grabbed me by the arm with a vice-like grip. The girl was amazingly strong. She was obviously taking charge, as she was prone to do.

Robin Sparrow was the loyal girl guide for me whenever I needed it, and this was clearly one of those times I needed her guidance. "Let's get the fuck out of here," she said, and only then did I realize that it was the end of the school day. That bell had indicated that school was over.

"The asshole deserved it, I'm sure," she said as she ushered me away from the buses and guided me like a blind person to the sidewalk leading away from our educational insane asylum. "But ever since I've known you, JFC, you've always had the subtle touch. There was nothing subtle about that."

"I admit, I got carried away. But somebody had to do something."

"Why then? Why that?"

I really didn't want to talk about it. "I really don't want to talk about it. But there was more to the story than meets the eye."

"There always is," she conceded. "I'm sure he deserved it, whatever *it* was."

"He did. But I'm now somewhat ashamed that I let my emotions take over. Something snapped inside, as my mother would say. Not good."

Just then a car drove by and an older student whom I recognized leaned out and shouted something indecipherable. But whatever it was, it was pretty nasty. The car behind him had another shouter who let go with "It's not over!"

Robin flipped the bird at him and made a face filled with contempt.

I knew it was not over. Not a chance of that. And the thought that all those viewers would think that my actions were unwarranted and extremely violent began to gnaw at my gut. Really, really not good. I'd been called an entire urban dictionary of insults about my appearance but never once had I been thought of as a violent offender.

"Oh shit," I said out loud.

"'Oh shit' is right," Robin echoed. "I'm taking you to the Recovery Room."

Chapter Six

The Recovery Room was in the basement of the Unitarian Church on Hemming Street. Robin had taken me there many times before. She called it her "home away from home."

This is because Robin was a drug addict, a bright young woman stupid enough to allow herself to graduate from beer to weed to ecstasy and on up to an array of heavy-duty painkillers, all during a single academic year. I was such a piss-poor friend that she did this right under my nose and my policy of non-interference was no help at all. I thought it was just a phase she had to go through, but it nearly killed her.

Then she found her way to the basement of the church and to a group of people she just called the Group—mostly adults who were addicted to one thing or another who got together several times a week to lend mutual support to any one of them having a bad day. No one would have guessed that someone like Robin—smart, savvy, worldly wise—would be an addict. But that's the way it went.

In order for me to be accepted by the Group, I had to have an addiction and, of course, I admitted to having an addiction to food. It wasn't just the grilled cheese sandwiches with the bread buttered on both sides and the perfect commingling of Gouda, Cheddar and Monterrey Jack melted right into the bread. I did have an overzealous thing for food in general, and the result was yet another overweight boy on this wobbly planet.

A couple of the members of the Group protested and said my food addiction didn't count, but Reverend Kevin Kimball said it didn't matter. I was welcome any time.

And this was one of those times.

As we walked down the cement stairway into the basement, I heard a driver hammering on his car horn and then somebody else was shouting some kind of insult at me, but Robin reached out and covered my ears as she guided me through the door.

As usual, there was Christian folk music drifting across the room. I recognized Bertrand, the ornately-tattooed metalhead who was a regular; Bob, the retired family court judge; and, of course, Reverend Kevin. Rev Kev, as he liked to be called.

The reverend greeted us and thanked us for coming. He didn't come out and ask why we were there because that wasn't his style. He was all about being non-judgmental and making the Recovery Room an open and accepting environment for anyone who needed it. And he could tell at least one of us needed it now.

"How was school?" he asked, looking first at me and then at Robin.

Neither of us answered, but Robin took out her phone and showed Rev Kev the thirty-second video.

"Oh dear," he said, looking compassionately at me. "I

think we should have something to eat."

Now you wouldn't think a recovery counsellor would offer a food addict food. But Reverend Kevin claimed to understand everything about addiction. He himself had been a gambling addict and had nearly bankrupted the Unitarian congregation with his online gambling habits.

He walked us into the kitchen and gave Robin and me a really delicious samosa that he heated up in the microwave. He didn't say another word until we finished eating and were licking our fingers.

Then Robin spotted the black kettle weights in the corner, picked them up and began doing those endless lifts she was so fond of.

"Do either of you want to talk about it?" the Rev finally asked.

"He doesn't want to talk about it," Robin answered for me. She did have a habit of doing that, but it often saved me from having to answer for myself, which is perfectly fine in my book.

"If you can't talk about it, you can't deal with it," Rev Kev said. He was prone to issuing clichés as adults so often do when they think they are offering advice.

"...seven one thousand, eight one thousand, nine one thousand," Robin chanted as she hefted those shiny kettle weights.

I took a deep breath. The samosa had at once calmed me down, steadied my nerves and somehow bribed me into realizing I had to tell someone what had prompted me to assault Larkin.

"Twelve one thousand, thirteen one thousand..."

"Okay," I said. "It went like this."

Robin stopped in mid-lift and set the weights back down on the concrete floor. The reverend stopped wiping the counter with a dish cloth and said, "If you don't mind, would you be willing to share it with the Group?" Reverend Kevin was really big on "sharing" and especially this "Group" thing.

I agreed and he led us back into the Recovery Room.

Bertrand saw that something was up and turned off the Christian folk music. Bob the Job—the honourable Judge Robert Preston—jumped up and put a handful of chairs in a circle. Kevin guided me to a seat and, as I could have predicted, handed me a foot-long birch tree branch that I knew to be the Talking Stick. So I now had my small audience which would, in the vernacular of the recovering addict therapy handbook, "bear witness" to my actions.

As Bertrand fidgeted with his nose ring and Judge Bob held a shaky cup of coffee halfway to his lips, Robin nodded and poked an elbow gently into my paunch to get me started.

"Okay, okay. It was like this," I began. "Gym class was over. We were in the locker room, most of us still in our underwear or half-dressed. Brady, a little guy who can never keep his mouth shut, calls Larkin an asshole for knocking his feet out from under him when we were playing dodgeball. Larkin just smiles at first like it doesn't bother him at all.

"But then, suddenly, Larkin turns and throws himself at Brady, slamming him head-first into the brick wall. Brady bounces off the wall and then falls to the floor, where Larkin pounces on him, grabs him by the hair and pounds his head into the concrete floor.

"Larkin leans back and is about to kick Brady in the stomach when I realize I have to do something. Everyone else is just standing and watching."

"Everyone but Harrison, apparently," Robin added.

"Harrison must have a pretty good reaction time," I continued, "because he has his phone out and is capturing the whole deal."

I turned to Robin and let her finish the story. "So Harrison posted it right away. Not the whole thing, of course. Just JFC pushing Larkin up against his locker, holding him there."

"And then giving him a rather serious head butt." As I said that last part, I felt another twinge of embarrassment.

There—I said it.

Bertrand was the first to speak. "So you got the creep to back off and you did what needed to be done."

"Only problem is," the judge chimed in, spilling some of his coffee on the floor as he cleared his throat, "what the viewers on the internet see is only John Francis attacking this Larkin turd."

"That's right," I said. "And so now the shit has hit the fan."

I was expecting some choice platitudes from Reverend Kevin, but that wasn't the case. He looked at me with great compassion and said, "And what are you going to do now?"

I took a deep breath and thought hard about it. There really was only one solution. "I'm going to go home and eat," I said. It's what an addict does. But I didn't say that part.

Everyone in the room nodded. "We have your back," Bertrand said, but I didn't really know what that meant in this situation.

"You can come back any time you like, any time you need us," the Rev said. "Door's open 24/7. Coffee's always on." But then he paused and added, "Fridge is usually stocked." And everyone laughed a somewhat uncomfortable snicker.

Then the Rev got a bit biblical. "This too shall pass," he said, "in the fullness of time."

And I really liked that last part. *The fullness of time*. It reminded me of feeling the great satisfaction of being full like after a real Thanksgiving turkey dinner. (Not that I'd had many of them in my life, but the TV image was often there in my dreams and in my mind-wandering moments at school.)

I felt better as Robin nodded towards the basement door and I stood up to leave. Judge Bob walked my way as I stretched my legs and involuntarily placed my hands upon my stomach. He set his shaky coffee cup down (the one with the words "Justice is Blind. Glasses are Not Enough") and laid a fatherly hand on my shoulder. "Larkin is Henry Kelsey's kid, isn't he?"

I nodded.

"Henry Kelsey is one of the meanest son of a bitch criminal lawyers I've ever seen in my courtroom. And he's good. Good like a snake under a child's bed. I've watched him set violent men free and smile at me. Your classmate Larkin probably grew up getting the crap beat out of him by his old man. I'd bet you good money on that. That devil of a lawyer is gonna want a piece of you. You're going to need more than Bertrand looking after your back." And then he gave me a hug.

I walked out of there with Robin, feeling I had allies. A weirder little band of addict allies could not be found, I am sure. But I felt thankful. A worried boy in an unfair world needs all the allies he can muster.

Robin was more than a little agitated as she reverted to one of her Save-JFC lectures. "I'm going to insist you start coming with me to Hard Bodies. I can be your trainer. We need to toughen you up for your own good. Turn some of that weight into muscle. You'd really like the elliptical and I bet you'd love training. Once you got your head around it."

"Maybe," I said for the one hundredth time. "Maybe I should," I repeated, knowing I wouldn't.

"Damn. I could use a joint right now," Robin said, and I knew the craving came to her because of this situation with me. "Lucky me. Just as soon as weed becomes legal, I discover I can't smoke it anymore because then I either want to toke up all day or move on to something heavier."

"Come over to my house," I said, "and we'll watch some old Arnold Schwarzenegger movies."

When my mother discovered Robin (my only real friend in the Northern or Southern Hemisphere) liked old Arnie movies, she bought an ancient VCR and a stash of second-hand videos from the Salvation Army store. She'd sit and watch them with us as we ate bacon-flavoured popcorn.

"Not today," she said. "I got to go to the gym and go to it until I burn."

I knew she'd say that. Muscle burn. Brain burn. Burn away all the bad thoughts with exercise. It was her way.

She looked antsy again. She wanted to run. "You gonna be okay?" she asked.

"I'm gonna be fine," I said. "Run."

And run she did. Like the wind.

As I walked on home alone, I kept thinking about how quickly Harrison's video would be spreading from a small circle of his friends, spiralling ever outward into the wider world where who knows how many strangers would be thinking I was nothing but a nasty piece of work. Many would even think, *I've seen the enemy and that is him in boxer shorts*.

Chapter Seven

So I don't suppose this is all that exciting in terms of telling a story unless it turned out that this all-too-classic locker room brawl was leading up to the worst time of my life. I understand that good stories these days are about young people like me getting into a tight place and coming out of it smelling like roses. As one famous writer once said, "It was the best of times, it was the worst of times."

Even that isn't quite appropriate. It all just turned out much different from what you or I could have expected. Difficult yes, but that makes it justifiable for the telling, does it not?

So what happened next?

I went home.

I told my mother what happened. When I held back and didn't tell my mother about things in my life, she always found out anyway and would get mad at me for not telling her myself. Besides, she had already seen Harrison's video on her newsfeed.

"I was only half-watching," she said, "when I said to myself, God damn, isn't that my John Francis? And there you were, pounding some boy up against a locker. I then said to myself, there must be a good reason for this. But I was also glad that you had on decent underwear. I don't know what people would think if you had on frayed or dirty underwear. They'd wonder what kind of mother sends her son to school in raggedy unwashed boxer shorts."

My mother said this while making me (I guess you saw this coming) a grilled cheese sandwich. Bread toasted, buttered meticulously on two sides, three kinds of cheese, amalgamated just so, sandwich flipped over and over to keep from burning. Heavy frying pan lid lifted and closed in an almost-religious manner.

I had to explain for a second time the whole sequence of events before she had the picture clearly in her head and, as I ate, slowly, inevitably, completely, I could see the anger building up in her. My mother was a person who could not contain her rage well. This had been an issue for a long time. Probably had something to do with the Invisible Man, my father, departing for parts unknown. There had been other problems too. Violence over parking spaces at Walmart. That incident with the dog, its ignorant owner and the flowerbed full of tulips by the sidewalk. Her boss at Dan the Pirate's Seafood Palace. (That one was rather ugly with a live lobster being taken from a giant glass tank and tossed around the room at dining patrons leading to her immediate dismissal.)

She now explored how we might get some kind of revenge on both Harrison and especially Larkin. Mom had a couple of social media accounts, under aliases, where she'd post unkind messages about people she didn't like. One was under the pseudonym of Mandy Howell and she had posted a picture of some other woman (who turned out to be a

Russian porn star) as her own photo, which brought her many, many followers. The other one was of a more mundane Viola Goodrich, who was supposedly a housewife somewhere in the Midwest. She'd written mean comments and even reposted insulting images of politicians, neighbours, the mayor, several police officers and even my disappearing father, only to discover that the internet world was vastly populated by people who simply loved to read terrible things about other people—whether they knew them or not.

So I had to explain to Mom not to do this. It would not make her any happier.

By this point, she had finished cleaning up the frying pan and had picked up the baseball bat from behind the door. It was an old wooden one she had bought at—where else?—the Sally Ann. A Louisville Slugger, to be exact. Louisville, in case you are wondering, is in Kentucky and it is famous for the manufacture of wooden baseball bats.

Mom had seen this exact model in an old country music video. I can't remember who they were, but it was a girl band from the South, all pretty and blonde, and the song was about a guy who had cheated on his girlfriend and she was getting revenge on his car with a Louisville Slugger. The first time we came across this, watching a marathon of country music videos, Mom said to me, "That must feel good. Really, really good."

It took us several months of scouring second-hand stores, but we finally found one, and she had cherished it ever since. The only time she put it into use was when a collection agency made the mistake of actually sending someone to our door. Fortunately, the young man knew how to duck, dive and run for his life.

Now she held the weapon in her hands and studied the grain of the wood. "They're going to try to kick you out of school now. You know that, don't you?"

"Put the bat down," I insisted. "I'm going to talk to Brady."

"Brady? What good will that do?"

"I'll ask Brady to speak to someone in the office. To tell them what really happened. Maybe this will all blow over." But I doubted that would be the case.

In order to get my mom to calm down, I sat with her and watched *Terminator* and *Terminator 2* back to back, although neither was my favourite. I had homework to do and I did it under the covers with a flashlight later that night, when I was sure my mom wasn't going to go outside the house on some kind of revenge rampage. Sometimes, watching a good solid revenge movie would get that out of her system. Sometimes not.

It might surprise you to learn that, once my math and science homework was finished, I slept rather well. My mother says I would sleep through the apocalypse, but I'm hoping it doesn't come to that. But if it does, sleep seems as good a way to experience the end of the world as any.

Sleep is a beautiful thing in a life of turmoil and unfairness. Sleep is an equalizer...and so much more. But don't get me going.

Chapter Eight

When I wake in the morning, I have a bad feeling about the day. But that is fairly common in my world.

I make a quick list of what I need to do:

1. Get up.
2. Eat something—preferably French toast or a reasonable, four-egg cheese omelette.
3. Accept the fact that there are no eggs in the house and suck it up.
4. Be kind to my mom and tell her what a wonderful day it is shaping up to be.
5. Get myself out the door.
6. Walk the four blocks to school. (Maybe if we lived further from the school, the longer walk would have been enough exercise to put me in better shape.)
7. Don't grieve over parental decisions.
8. Pretend it's going to be a regular day of school.
9. Return to a calm state of being.
10. Watch the looks my fellow classmates throw at me as I wait for more shit to hit the fan.

I decide not to plan my day any further.

I don't even have a chance to sit in my seat in first period math when Mrs. Traeger pulls me aside and says I am wanted in the office. I nod and she looks at me with the look that clearly and silently states, "I know what you did."

I try to look back with a look that says, "No, you don't," but probably I instead have the demeanour of one of those "dead man walking" criminals on the way to an execution.

On my brief, purposefully-soulful and plodding trek to the office, I ponder, as many before me had, how the internet and all the paraphernalia of social media have been a curse more than a blessing. They are powerful tools of knowledge and interconnectivity but also guns in the hands of what Robin likes to call the unkindsters.

So, even as I am slowing my pace in hopes that it will somehow deter the inevitable, I can sense someone quickly approaching me from behind. Classes have already started, so it's either someone late for their dreaded French class or more probably someone wanting a piece of me.

"Hold up, cowboy."

I realize at once it is the familiar, slightly nasal but oh-so-welcome voice of the Robin bird.

I turn and the girl, angel disguised as a former-druggie-now-vegan hopeful world saver, gives me a hug that nearly knocks the breath out of me. Then she looks me right in the eye. "Office?"

I nod.

"I'm going with you."

And suddenly the dark morning blossoms into song. "I don't know if they'll allow it."

"I'll insist."

"But you know what Morgan can be like."

Morgan is Mr. Mantel Morgan, our not-so-beloved principal. He's a we're-going-to-have-to-send-a-message-to-the-student-body-with-your-disciplinary-action kind of administrator. He came straight out of the military into education, and that should tell you something. Despite his civilian role, on his morning announcements and at the all-too-occasional auditorium gatherings, he uses words like "insubordination," "decorum," "esprit de corps" and the dreaded "zero tolerance."

"You need a student advocate. That's me. Student Council officially approved it last year. Morgan never said yes or no to it, so I'll play that card."

"I never knew of Student Council actually doing anything worthwhile."

"There are exceptions. This was one. The advocate thing was my idea. Just never had a chance to apply it."

"God, I love being a guinea pig."

"And I love being the first student advocate of this god-forsaken school."

"God bless you," I say, a term I borrowed from one of my mom's favourite revenge movies, the Clint Eastwood one called *Gran Torino*.

"I thought you said you didn't believe in God."

"I do now."

We arrive at the gallows and walk in. The secretary, Mrs. Laughlin, frowns at the two of us. "I guess I'm here to see Mr. Morgan," I say.

"You're out of luck. He's off to a conference. It's Mr. Battle who wants to see you."

"Mr. Battle?" I am not out of luck after all. Mr. Battle is a puppy dog compared to Morgan the Mean.

"Yes. Go right in. But not her," she says, pointing to my ally.

"I'm his student advocate," Robin asserts.

"What the hell is that?" Mrs. L snaps back.

"I'm going with him."

At that, Laughlin just shrugs and says, "Whatever," a phrase she had obviously heard so many times from ne'er-do-well youth coming to the office for chastisement that it simply stuck with her and echoed out of her head when a time like this rolled around.

Mr. Battle. I can't believe my luck.

Mr. Lawrence Battle is one of the two vice-principals who had been at Memorial High since the beginning of time as far as I could tell. He is at least sixty-five years old and no one else working at the school is even a day over fifty. Teachers here burn out early or late, but they tend to burn out or give out or get tired and want to rest or just leave classrooms behind and do anything but lecture and take flak from young punks like my rowdy colleagues.

But not Mr. B.

The door to his office is open, as always. We walk in.

There he sits at his old oak desk in a warm pool of morning sunlight. He is looking out the window at some clouds floating by and, when he hears us come in, he swivels around. He has fingers tented in front of him, complemented by a look on his face that said he was at peace with the world, or, at least, with the small parcel of real estate that comprised his school office.

It was well known that Lawrence Garrison Battle is what many referred to as an aging hippie, although most of us didn't really know what a real hippie was. That was so far before our time. The beatific (a word I picked up on the Word-of-the-Day website) smile on his face is probably something left over from his stoner days back in the early 1970s. He has one of those awful grey-hair ponytails, held together with a mere rubber band, probably from his desk drawer.

I think that the school board had tried to mandatorily retire the old dude in the past. At least that was the rumour, but he had invoked some kind of discrimination clause or other and hung onto his desk, his job and his basic respect for teenagers, despite the mounting evidence that we are far more trouble than we are worth.

"John Francis," he says. "And Robin, is it?"

"Robin Sparrow."

"An honour to have you both in my humble office," he says, smiling enigmatically.

I had developed a nervous blink in the bright sun and, noticing this, Mr. B. tugs his shade down a little. "Better?"

"Much. Thanks," I say.

He looks at Robin, opens up his hands and shrugs. "What brings her along for the ride?"

"Student advocate," she answers.

"Right on. I remember. I supported the Student Council on this, as I recall, but it was all shot to hell by the school board. Anyway, you are welcome here even though this is about John Francis."

"Thank you," Robin says.

"Well," he says, turning to me, "I guess you know why you are here. We seem to have a bit of a situation."

I like his innocuous choice of the word. It is truly, if nothing else, a situation.

"There were mitigating circumstances," Robin shoots back. Just like her to use a word like mitigating.

Mr. B tugs at his ponytail once and flips his fingers out to each side. "I understand. Nothing on the internet is really exactly as it appears. Nothing. I've learned in my significantly many years that *nothing* in life is really as it appears. But we still have this, um, situation we have to deal with."

"You've seen the video?" I ask naïvely.

"It was shown to me. I would not have sought it out on my own. But I've seen it and, dare I say, the entire town has seen it. Comments seem to come from all four corners of the globe as well, I'm afraid to say. In one sense, it's really quite amazing that the video has travelled so far. But give it to me straight. What actually transpired?"

He leans forwards in a most non-threatening manner and I tell him what happened and how. You clearly don't need to hear it again.

"Ah," Lawrence Garrison Battle says. "For Larkin Kelsey, what goes around comes around. He reaped what he sowed."

Clichés, I know, but these are better than an outright lecture.

"Why didn't Brady step forward and state that you were coming to his defence?"

Before I can say anything, my student advocate answers, "Because Brady thinks he'll look like a snivelling trouble-making twerp if he tells the truth."

"And you say Harrison caught most of the entire episode on his phone?"

"He did," I say. "But as you saw, he only posted the last bit."

"The one with you doing a full-body press on Larkin and that unfortunate head thing. Where'd you learn that move anyway?"

"My mom likes to watch UFC on TV. Sometimes she makes nachos and we sit and do a mini marathon. Some of that stuff they do just sort of sinks in."

"Nachos" Mr. Battle responds. "I like nachos. But never had much of a taste for fighting."

"Me neither to be honest."

"I didn't think so. You never struck me as the violent type."

When he says it, he sort of smiles and I wonder if there was some aging-hippie small linguistic joke there by using "struck" and "violent" in the same sentence. Larry Battle is legendary around the school for his obtuse, strange and probably hippie sense of humour.

Robin jumps in. I was almost enjoying the conversation but she can be impatient at times. "Mr. Battle, could we cut to the chase and you tell us why John Francis was called down here?"

"Of course." He clears his throat the way all adults do when they wanted to make a point. "Larkin's father has gone to the police over this. Based on the evidence presented to them—including the video, of course—the police are considering pressing charges. The school police liaison officer has come to us with the situation before proceeding further. She wanted to be present but I asked to have a chat with you first. So here we are. I'm hoping we can head this off. It would be bad karma all around."

"And no one wants bad karma," Robin says.

I am trying to remember exactly *what* karma was from my many discussions with my Buddhist neighbour. It always seemed to be one of those vague, overused words that could mean whatever you wanted it to mean.

Many things are going through my head. Despite the fact that Mr. Battle seems to be trying to keep the whole meeting as low-key and casual as he can, now that I knew the police are involved, the skinny little boy still skipping down the sidewalk of my brain has stopped dead in his tracks and is ready to scream.

"What exactly am I being charged with?"

"Mr. Kelsey has gone to the police with the video and asking them to charge you with assault," Mr. Battle says.

Robin's jaw drops. Mine remains frozen in place.

"But there were witnesses to the whole event," Robin blurts out. "The police won't charge him if they know the whole story."

"So you need to get those witnesses to come forward. Send them here first. How many were in that aisle of the locker room at that minute?"

I try to think. "Six or seven. But the one who needs to speak up is Brady."

Mr. Battle picks up the phone. "Shall I get the secretary to call him down here?"

"No. Let me talk to him first."

"Okay, but I can only hold off that meeting with the police until this afternoon. Talk to Brady and I'll get Harrison in here to see if I can get him to hand over the full video."

But I know that Harrison has almost certainly deleted the full video. What the world knew was just what was posted as if *that* was the whole truth of the matter.

The word *assault* echoes loudly in my brain. Despite the fact that such an accusation would run counter to everything that anyone ever knew about me—the gentle, easygoing, funny, almost annoyingly-polite overweight kid —I understand that people like to believe bad things about other people. This is especially true in high school.

The VP turns to his computer screen and punches a couple of keys on the keyboard. "First period is about to end. Brady should be leaving Room 234 in a few minutes. I should probably get him down here right away, but go ahead and talk to him first. If he comes to us voluntarily, that would be the best scenario."

As we leave, Robin takes my hand, something she had never done before. Hers is downright sweaty and I realize that she is afraid for me. "Let's go find Brady," she says.

But I stop in my tracks. I knew Brady and I knew that two of us would be worse than one. Brady was indeed one of those people who thought the worst of almost anyone. I'd heard more often than once what he had to say about Robin. Brady had called her a "freak of nature" and other cruel things. I don't want Robin to have to endure any other malicious things he might say to her.

"No, I gotta do this on my own," I say.

Robin lets go of my hand and looks straight into my eyes.

"You're sure?"

"I'm sure," I say even though I'm not sure of anything. The rules of the universe, the rules of my world, my understanding of where I fit into the great scheme of things, had changed. I am in uncharted territories, "uncharted waters", as I'd heard someone say. And I will either sink or swim.

I want to think that it would be up to me. That I can bring forth the truth and set things right. But I know that isn't the case. It's up to what everyone *believes* is the truth about JFC.

Robin gives me a hug and a reassuring look and then hangs back as I trudge off to find Brady coming out of Room 234. As the bell begins to ring for changing classes, I am suddenly hungry.

If only I had something to eat.

Chapter Nine

I've known Brady since we were both ten years old. He never liked me very much, but then Brady didn't really like anyone that much.

He had a dog back then, an Irish setter, I think, and, as I recall, he claimed he loved that dog more than anything in the world. But he mistreated it something awful.

At school he was picked on by a range of the more belligerent brats that we all had to put up with. Brady had always been at the low end of the pecking order, it seemed to me. He pretended, however, that he was not at the lowest end, so he kept trying to find someone else to pick on. He tried me, but I was already developing my behavioural coating of Teflon. His insults never really got to me. I'd agree that I was this or that and then turn it into a joke. He was pretty easy to deal with, but always pretty hard to like.

As he grew older, he developed in an odd way—growing bolder by the year, finding ways to piss off just about anyone, even the bigger guys who used him as a whipping boy whenever they could. I'd come to his defence over the years, using my best pre-Zen tactics to try to defuse situations, but Brady usually turned against me, too. It was in his nature.

But we're older now, so he should be reasonable, right?

Wrong.

"Brady, we have to talk," I say.

"Nothing to talk about, fartface," he says. Funny that he can't come up with a better insult than that.

"This thing in the locker room. Are you willing to go down to Battle's office with me and tell him what really happened?"

He is walking away from me. Other kids are watching. "No," he says. "N.O. spells no."

That's when I notice the bruise on his cheek and the goose egg on his forehead, where Larkin had pounded his head on the concrete floor. "But if I didn't stop him, Larkin could have really hurt you."

"Get away, asswipe. You don't know what you're talking about."

I have to hustle to keep up with him. "Brady. Dammit. Larkin's father will convince the police to press charges against me. I need your help." I suppose you could say I was begging.

Brady stops and stares at me. It's a look of pure contempt. Suddenly, I am the enemy. I am just another in a long string of harassers and tormentors.

More begging is clearly required. "Brady, I need someone to help me tell the truth."

"Nobody gives a shit about the truth, stupido. And I'm not the one in the video, am I?"

And with that he's gone. Strike one.

I have no other choice but to stand there with a river of my classmates arcing around me like I'm a rock in a stream, all of them giving me their facial opinion of a classmate who had proven himself to be some kind of violent monster.

I guess all along I believed I could smooth-talk, shuffle and make my way through high school and come out the other end somewhat normal, ready to eventually lose a few pounds, use my wit and wisdom to go on to university, get a reasonably good job in an office and live a somewhat normal life.

But yesterday had changed all that.

The traffic in the hall is thinning. I decide to simply go to class. That's when I feel a rough hand on my shoulder.

I turn, half expecting it to be Larkin. Instead, it's Harrison. A worried-looking Harrison.

"We need to talk," he says, using almost the same words I had said to Brady.

"I could use your help, you know," I snap back. "Your little video has me up shit creek without a paddle."

"I know," he says. "It was a mistake. I got carried away. My parents are really pissed."

"Can't you take it down?"

"I could, but it won't go away. It's been forwarded…everywhere."

"What about the unedited version?"

"I don't have it anymore," he admits. Just like I figured.

"But you only posted the bit where I was pounding Larkin."

"Like I said, I no longer have the rest. I wasn't thinking."

"Now what?"

"Now I don't know what to do." He seems downright sorry for his actions. This doesn't seem at all like the Harrison I know. Harrison rarely instigated treachery, but he loved to be on the sidelines, egging on whomever was in the mood for nastiness, and he had a signature snicker and a gleam in his eye that were archetypical for his kind. In recent years, he'd thrown a few lame overweight insults my way, but only as part of a posse of his like-minded louts, of which there were plenty. Followers of the wolf pack, picking over the meaty bones of the victims after the predators had had their fill.

"The cops are coming to speak to me later today," I tell Harrison. "Go down to Mr. Battle and tell him what you saw. Tell him you posted only part of the fracas."

He looks a little puzzled at the word.

"The fight. Tell him what happened before I went after Larkin."

"I can't."

"Why not?"

"Larkin's father. He already came to my house and talked to my dad. He threatened to sue my family because I posted what I did and he claimed I could even be charged for posting it. He was there in my living room talking like a big-ass lawyer."

"He *is* a big-ass lawyer."

"He said he would do anything to protect his son. When I explained that Larkin had been beating on Brady, he said I was lying, and if I said that to anyone else, he'd make sure my entire family was punished."

"How could he do that?"

"I don't know. But it scared the shit out of my father. He doesn't have money to defend me in some kind of court case. So I gave him my phone with the original. He's got the only copy."

"Except for the shortened version on the internet which will remain there well after our lifetime."

"I suppose. I feel bad for you, but what can I do?"

"Go speak to Battle."

"I can't. Sorry."

I'd never heard Harrison apologize for anything in his life. I don't think anyone else ever had either. In the midst of the shit show of my day, it's a kind of golden moment.

But we're late for class. "Gotta run," Harrison says. And run he does.

I walk in late for Mr. Powell's class, but he doesn't say a word. I take my seat by the window and wonder yet again why these moulded school desks don't allow for a little more wiggle room for us plus-size students who, according to the news reports, are accounting for more and more of the teenage population of this supersized nation.

Aside from Robin, I expect to find no allies among the boys and girls I'd grown to know over the years. I even think maybe I should cut Robin free, set her adrift, before I drag her down to the depths with me.

And where, in fact, would this all lead? At first, I half-thought it would just blow over, but now that Larkin's father and the police are involved, I don't know. Henry Larkin is a locally famous criminal lawyer with a penchant for garnering TV news time spouting highly-convincing diatribes about the innocence of his clients—mostly white-collar embezzlers and outright thieves of the grand theft variety, but also the occasional high-profile murder suspect.

As my mind drifts and I stare at the comforting branches

of an ancient white birch near the school parking lot, I start wondering how this all is going to affect my mother. There has to be some way I can sort this out on my own without bringing her into it. She's unpredictable and mercurial, and absolutely anything might happen. I know she wouldn't really take it out on me. She never does. But look out, world.

I take a deep breath, decide to come in from the topmost branches of the birch tree and take a chance on looking around the room, just to see how badly everyone thinks of Memorial High's currently most notorious criminal.

As soon as I do that, the heads turn my way—not all at once, but one at a time, like it was some well-choreographed scene in a low-budget horror movie. The looks go like this:

1. disgust
2. revulsion
3. loathing
4. repugnance

I make a mental note that my Word-of-the-Day internet research has brought fruitful results.

But then I see a flicker of a smile on a girl's face. Is it another Brady-like sideways smirk of contempt? Of course.

But after a couple more simple acts of facial aversion, I see Martha Delano give me what seems to be a genuine smile and a thumbs-up. Debating Club Martha, who has considerable brains to go with her feminine beauty.

Am I possibly missing something in the look? No, in fact, she holds my gaze without looking away. And then there comes a second look from none other than basketball star Brad Smollett. A head nod. Another thumbs-up. Then two more head nods (the positive kind) from kids I barely know.

If I had the forethought, I would have tried to keep a mental scorecard. The nays still far outweigh the yays, but the sunlight streaming into the classroom between the branches of the beautiful birch tree suddenly seems much warmer, much brighter. I would at least have a few fans to weep and moan at my imminent crucifixion and that takes a fair amount of weight off my shoulders and makes me think I have good reason to see the drama through to its inevitable end with dignity.

And then, somehow, the whole damn problem just goes away.

Chapter Ten

Well, no, it doesn't. I just pretended that was the case as a kind of thought experiment.

That overly optimistic thought lasts not much more than five or six nanoseconds and then it is gone. But over the years I had practised such positive acts of imagination to keep my childhood fantasy life alive and well as I progressed beyond my preteen tenure and headed into the turbulent double-digit years.

I had often fantasized about having two happy, mentally-healthy parents. I had conjured up wealth that seemed to drop out of the sky. I had willed several very likeable and lovely girls to fall in love with me and be my girlfriends—sequentially, of course; I had no ambition to be a teenage Casanova. I imagined once that I had suddenly lost weight overnight and woke in the morning feeling fit and looking damn good in the mirror, if I do say so myself. At other times, I was just the guy at school that everyone wanted to have for a best friend.

But those were all daydreams, fantasies, alternate realities that may well exist on that promised other plane of existence.

As class continues, I stare at the tree. God, I love that old birch tree. So tall, so grand, so non-judgmental.

And then there's this: what if I just get up in the middle of class, walk out the classroom door, stride (well, shuffle) down the hall and leave the building? I would then simply walk away from it all. I wouldn't go home and I wouldn't return to school. I'm not the suicidal type, as I feel that people who even toy with self-inflicted death are way too drama-driven, far too self-absorbed and selfish. So that would never ever be me.

No, I could just leave. Go somewhere. Make it all go away. Start a new life with a new identity in another town. Lose a little weight. Change my hair colour, maybe. I always wanted to have reddish hair like Ed Sheeran. So why the fuck not?

I'm old enough to get a job at McDonald's but I guess that would put me too close to all those salty fries and Big Macs. But certainly there would be other jobs for an overweight sixteen-year-old high school dropout with no employment experience whatsoever. It's a large country. Somebody would be desperate enough to hire me somewhere.

I could live at the Salvation Army until I had enough money to rent my own place. It would be a dilapidated rat hole of an apartment at first, with a single-burner hotplate, a small, noisy refrigerator, cracks in the stippled ceiling and cockroaches. But that would build character.

I couldn't quite envision what town this would be, but it would be maybe just an hour's bus ride away. An industrial city, probably with litter in the streets and uncaring people up and down the sidewalks. But that didn't matter, because it would only be a first step to a new life.

C'mon. Tell me truthfully you never thought about going out the door—you know which door I mean—and just walking away? Sure you have. Everyone has. But I have a better reason than most to do so.

I let the fantasy linger. Bus ride. Crappy but paying job. Shitty apartment. Uncaring citizens. Me sitting in my pyjamas at ten o'clock at night, watching old Kung Fu movies that pretended to have spiritual meaning on my laptop. Undoubtedly, I'd be eating something healthy.

No, that somehow threw it all off. I would not be watching *Kung Fu Kid* and chowing down on several stalks of celery with a Granny Smith apple for a chaser. That possibility completely destroyed my potential, mythological life. I would be eating chips. Or an overly-toasted grilled cheese sandwich that I just burned in the frying pan on that semi-functional one-burner hot plate.

That's what I would be doing.

I suddenly see a man's hand curled into a fist. It is not about to hit me, but instead, its tapping on my desk. Mr. Powell.

"Hello in there," he says.

"Oops," I muster.

"You like my class so much that you decided to stay even after everyone left?" He doesn't even sound sarcastic.

"I'm sorry. I guess I drifted."

"I understand. You have a lot on your mind."

I start to unwedge myself from the entrapment of the welded desk-chair torture device but Mr. Powell waves a hand for me to stay put. "Next class will be in here in a few minutes, but can we talk?"

Mr. Powell seems compassionate. No sarcasm. No insinuation. No I'm-smarter-than-you-you-little-asshole tactics that are common among the meaner pedagogical professionals at Memorial. But then, Mr. Powell had always been a bit of a mystery to students, including me. He's one of those teachers who usually seem to have no personality at all. He has a forgettable face and a forgettable character and wears the same grey suit and grey tie every day. We always called him Mr. Whatshisname, even to his face.

But now I'm thinking, *Here is yet another adult being kind to me.*

"John Francis, what do your friends call you?"

"I only really have one friend."

"And what does that person call you?"

"John Francis. Everybody else calls me JFC if they are reasonably kind. Otherwise, it's a range of names, if they choose to be unkind."

"You ever hear of the guy they call the Planet Walker?"

"No."

"Look him up. His name was John Francis. You'd like him. Maybe you're a little like him."

I'm not sure if that is a good or a bad thing, but I promise to look him up.

"Can I go now?" I ask, not that Mr. Powell is being unkind. I just need to get on with my day. Not the walking-out-the-door business, but the let's-get-serious-and-put-the-screws-to-me-soon business so we can get it over with.

"I'm sure you had a good reason to push Larkin into that locker door," he says. "Life is not always fair. In fact, it's almost never fair. My wife left me three days after we got married."

"Your wife?" I have no idea why he is telling me this.

"She said I was too boring and that she couldn't stand spending her life with a man as boring as me."

I can see her point, but what do I know about marriage? "Why did she marry you, then?"

"I asked her the same thing. She said she married me because she felt sorry for me."

What this has to do with my situation I have no idea, but it's an interesting conversation, given the circumstances, and I know Mr. Powell is trying to make a personal connection. So I reply, "Then maybe someday someone will marry me."

Perhaps that was an inappropriate thing to say, but I am not a master of teacher-student conversations. My thought was that if someone could marry you out of pity, then someday a woman might pity me enough to marry me and we'd live happily ever after, or at least for three days like Mr. Powell's marriage until the pity wore off and she left.

Mr. Powell looks puzzled for a few seconds, but then regroups, raps his knuckles on the desk and says, "You're not alone, John Francis. There are many more like us. Be strong. Hold your head up."

Other kids are filtering in now. Mr. Powell's little pep talk is over.

He goes back to his desk and I wiggle out of my seat, gather my books and walk out the door.

Unfortunately, Mr. Battle is right there, waiting for me.

"Showtime," he says. "Officer Foster is in my office. She wants to speak with you. I put her off as long as I could."

Chapter Eleven

Mr. Battle looks worried as he guides me down the hall to his office. "I had a call from the big guy and he's very concerned. He thinks this little feud between you and Larkin could blow up in our faces and make the school look really bad. Maybe affect our funding."

"There's no feud, Mr. Battle. You heard my story and that's the truth."

"I know. I know. But nowadays it's all about the optics."

"Well, it's my problem. Not the school's. No one will blame the school for this."

"You're wrong. Everyone will blame the school. And with the principal gone, everyone will blame me."

"What do you want me to do?"

Battle seems downright exasperated now. "Heck, John Francis, I don't know. Apologize?"

"Sure. I could do that." You have to remember, I come from a different realm of thought than most when it comes to solving problems. I'm in the whatever-gets-the-job-done school of thought. In the kingdom of cheese (which is my little fiefdom) there are no heroes. Only survivors. Or at least there were up until now.

My answer, however, seems to make Mr. Battle even more exasperated. His jaw muscles tighten and he holds his arms up with fingers outstretched in frustration. "No. Don't do it."

"What?"

"Don't do it. Don't apologize."

"Then what do you want me to tell this police liaison person?"

"I don't know. I don't want to see you hung out to dry, but I'd like to keep things from escalating."

"I'll see what I can do." I really do like Mr. B and don't want to see his job on the line. I am coming to the conclusion that whatever I would do, I'll be screwed anyway. So why drag down nice people with a sinking ship? That thought suddenly makes me feel a strong sense of kinship with the *Titanic*.

"Well, it's Brenda Jean Foster you'll be talking to. You know her as Officer Foster. You've seen her around the halls."

"BJ?"

"Is that what the kids call her?"

"Yeah."

BJ doesn't wear a uniform but everyone knows who she is and why she's there. She's young, probably only twenty-five if that, but she's still a cop. She wanders around between classes or haunts the hallways looking for kids selling weed or pills.

Any of the real hoodlums always know where she is in the school at any time. I think they have their own Facebook page or something to track her whereabouts. We don't have any major criminal activity at our school, really, but those wannabe pimps, pill pushers and weed merchants are a tight-knit bunch who were on top of the technology to keep an eye on the police liaison.

I think Brenda Jean has taken away a couple of knives and busted the son of a local real estate tycoon who tried to break into the drug biz on his own, but aside from that, she's just another adult who walks the halls, acting friendly and relatively cool with most kids. Like some teachers and other adults, she tries a little too hard at times, pretending to be one of us by saying things like "What up?" and "Chill," and her personal favourite, "Be cool, fool."

Obviously, she was nowhere near the boys' locker room the day the deal went down for me.

"John Francis, be careful what you say. Ms. Foster is acting awfully serious today."

At the office, Mr. B opens the door. BJ is sitting there in her uniform, with her back to me. She usually wears her really nice, long, auburn hair hanging down, but now it's tied up into a knot at the back of her head.

She turns as we walk in. "Good," she says.

Mr. Battle goes to sit down at his desk but she holds up a hand. "No. You have to leave."

"Why?" Mr. B looks shocked.

"I'm sorry. I was told that under no circumstances should anyone else be in the room except family."

"I don't see any family," Mr. B says, now looking more than a little miffed.

Officer Foster turns to me. "John Francis, we tried to contact your mother and father but couldn't locate them. We even went to your apartment and knocked on the door."

Of course. My mother wouldn't answer the door to a cop in a million years. "Well, my dad has been gone for a fairly long time. He sort of opted out of the marriage and the family. And my mom, well, she's been sick lately and staying with a friend until she's better." That part was a lie, of course.

"Then I should stay," Mr. B interjects.

"No," Brenda Jean says. "You leave. I sit here and speak to John Francis. This one will be off the record. I have my orders. You'll have to trust me on this."

Mr. Battle scowls and then gives me a look that says, *You okay with this*?

I nod. What do I have to lose?

Mr. B backs out of the office and closes the door.

I take a seat by the wall. This is where you sit if you're in trouble. Anyone who walks into the VP's office knows there are two chairs for students. One which you sit in if you want to talk to the VP about selecting the right university and the other if you've been called to the office because you're in trouble. I'm pretty sure Officer BJ isn't going to talk to me about my chances of getting into Harvard.

"No recording equipment, no wire on me, not even a notebook," she says, holding her hands up in the air.

The uniform throws me off, though. I'd seen her in it only a couple of times before, at official school functions. Now I notice she has a belt with a couple of leather cases attached —bear spray, maybe. A Taser. She doesn't have a gun, but she does have that cool-looking radio thing attached to her shoulder.

"I guess you know why you are here," she says. She is trying to sound tough. Well, she *does* sound tough; it just doesn't seem to fit with her. She has nice eyes and those high cheekbones my mom likes to point out when we watch old movies with glamorous women actors.

But Brenda Jean is trying to be all business, not some teenage boy's female cop fantasy. "I've seen the video."

"People in China have probably seen the video by now," I say.

"Excuse me?"

"It was just a joke. You know what I mean."

"But this isn't a laughing matter," she says, which really does sound like a line from one of those old movies. In fact, my own dear mother had borrowed that line and used it for any number of things that had gone wrong in our lives that we tried to find the humour in.

"I know."

"Just tell me what happened. Off the record."

I wonder exactly why this was "off the record." Who decides what is off the record and on the record and what exactly *is* the record, anyway? And isn't there usually one version of things that is real and one that is just the record, whether true or not?

I don't know. So I just tell her the story. My story.

When I have finished, she says, "I expected as much. Do you have any evidence indicating that's the way it played out?"

"No. Harrison caught most all of it on his phone, but he says he doesn't have the first part anymore."

"What about witnesses? Certainly others were in the locker room."

"No one is going to say they saw anything except me pushing Larkin up against the locker and giving him that love tap with my forehead." Robin had already talked to every one of the lads who had been in the locker room that day. No one wanted to be the snitch. I knew the code, and if anyone broke it, they'd probably get as much crap via social media as I was getting.

"Not even Brady?"

"Especially not Brady."

Officer Foster fidgets with that radio Velcroed to her uniform. Is she thinking of calling for backup?

"You want some water?" she suddenly asks. "I think you need some water."

"I'm okay."

But she gets up and walks out of the room and comes back no more than ninety seconds later with two bottles of water. "All they had was this flavoured stuff," she says, handing me one of the bottles.

Mine is watermelon-flavoured. Just to please her, I crack the plastic cap and take a slug. It tasted like crap and not at all like watermelon. Besides, who wants to drink water that tastes like fake watermelon while being interrogated by a police officer?

Well, *interrogated* is probably too big a word for our little chat. And she was polite enough to think that maybe I'm parched or nervous and need a beverage, a pick-me-up. It's just too bad she hadn't offered food.

I hold my crappy watermelon-flavoured water bottle in front of me so I could read the label: artificial flavouring. I know what that means. Robin had explained it to me more than once. Chemicals manufactured in a factory in New Jersey somewhere along the Jersey Turnpike.

Officer Brenda Jean looks at me a little funny. Maybe she thinks I'm about to make a toast. *Here's to solving this ever-expanding dilemma.* I actually think she's a bit lost for words and doesn't know what to say next.

Just then the door is wrenched open. It's Robin. She barges in, as is her style.

"What are you doing?" Brenda Jean blurts out. She has her hand on her pepper spray.

"I'm his student advocate. I have a right to be present."

Brenda Jean takes her hand off her pepper spray holster. "Student advocate?"

"Authorized by student council," Robin says. Boy, she is worked up.

"I already told Mr. Battle this had to be a private conversation."

"I know. He told me."

"I think you should leave."

"I think I should stay."

Good old Robin. Always trying to cover my back. I'm not sure I need it, but it feels good to have her here in the room to maybe take the edge off of an awkward situation for the police woman and me.

"Do you want her to stay?" BJ asks.

"Please," I say. "If you don't mind. She *was* authorized by student council."

Brenda Jean flips her fingers in the air. "Stay." And then she takes a slug of her bottled water, which I note is lemon-flavoured and has to taste better than watermelon. I wonder if she had purposefully given me the less desirable flavour.

Robin promptly sits down behind the desk where the VP usually sits. Then she gives me a dirty look and asks, "Why are you drinking that shit?"

I just shake my head.

Brenda Jean stirs uncomfortably. She looks at me and then at my advocate. "The real issue here, as far as I'm concerned, is that Larkin's father is likely to convince my superiors to press charges. He's made that clear. I expect he will come down to the station this afternoon and do so. If I know him, he'll make a big deal of it, bigger than it already is. He'll blame you. He'll blame the school, too. If I know him, he'll probably try to sue the school board, as well. These would be serious charges. You, John Francis, are old enough to be charged as an adult and that video is fairly damaging."

Robin blasts out of her seat. "That's fucking ridiculous."

Brenda Jean nods. "But that doesn't resolve the problem."

"Why don't I just apologize?" I offer again.

"You don't need to apologize," Robin asserts.

I had to admit she is a damn good student advocate, but clearly Brenda Jean isn't the enemy here.

"It could help," Brenda Jean says. I'm beginning to see that she, deep down, is a pragmatist. Like me.

"What kind of justice system is this anyway?" Robin demands. It wasn't a rhetorical question.

"An imperfect system," Brenda Jean admits. "But it's the only one we've got."

Chapter Twelve

Mr. Battle pokes his head in the door just then. BJ gives him a look that could fry meat.

"Just checking. Everything okay in here?"

BJ waves him into the room. "You can come in now. Just don't you and Miss Student Advocate gang up on me, okay, Larry?"

Mr. B slides into the room and pretends to adjust some books on the bookshelves. Robin is staring at him and I know she is about to launch into one of her grand raging tirades against "the system" or her personal favourite rant on the "systemic adult conspiracies."

But before she can get started, there is a blast of static and a raspy voice comes over BJ's two-way. "Henry Kelsey made his move. You'll have to bring the kid in. Over."

BJ unhitches her radio mic from her shoulder with that satisfying undoing-Velcro sound. "Copy that," she says. "Over."

"Processing clerk is out on another extended lunch so we'll have to hold him for a bit. Over."

"Damn, really? Over."

"Yes, damn, really. Over and out."

Mr. B's jaw drops. I am trying to make sense of what I just

heard and at the same time trying to find what Reverend Kevin would call my "happy place," that safe haven in your mind you can go to when you feel the welling of anxiety set in. Mine is my kitchen at home with the refrigerator door open and a full-to-overflowing fridge.

Trouble with going to that happy place is that it makes me hungry.

"Why don't you guys just use cell phones?" Mr. B blurts out. I can see his point. The whole radio thing does seem a bit like a really old cop show.

"I don't know. The guys just seem to like their radios. Some of them don't trust cell phones."

"I don't blame them," Robin states, "but what is this stuff about Larkin's father? What's he got to do with it?"

"He's been pressuring us to charge John Francis with assault. Now he's succeeded. We have to take John Francis in and go through the procedures. He'll have to go to court before a judge, but not today. We just need to book him." There's another one of those cop phrases.

Mr. Battle scrunches up his face. "I don't know if you have the authority to take him while school is still in session. I'll have to check with Principal Morgan and he's away in New Orleans on conference."

BJ gives him a look. "Please, Larry, don't make this any harder than it already is."

"I'm okay, really," I say. "Don't worry about me."

"I'm going with him," Robin insists.

BJ says, "No, you're not. And just everyone calm down. Let me do my job."

"Oh, right," Robin snarls. "That's what the Nazi soldiers

said, wasn't it?"

Leave it to Robin to take it all over the top.

"I'm okay," I say. I hold out my wrists, trying to be cooperative. I'm sure there will be handcuffs involved and I had always wondered what they actually felt like.

"Don't be ridiculous. Come on, John Francis."

Robin is still protesting when BJ walks me out of the office, her hand gripping my arm.

I think for a split second about bolting. There would be, after all, dozens of kids watching a pepper-spray-armed, two-way-radio woman cop in uniform walking one of their plus-size classmates down the dark hall and that was pretty good entertainment for an otherwise dull Tuesday afternoon. The handcuffs would have been way more cool. But at least I have Robin behind me shouting obscenities for a soundtrack, calling BJ names that she must have been inventing on the spot. Pretty good drama, pretty cool soundtrack.

I think BJ is finding it terribly uncomfortable and I myself switch from isn't-this-cool mode to damn-I-wish-I-had-tucked-in-my-shirt mode. I try to walk like Sean Penn in that movie my mom had made me watch called *Dead Man Walking*. I guess I should be more scared, but I'm thinking that whatever goes down the pike from here, however things turn out, no one will ever look at me the same again.

The police cruiser is parked right in front of the school. BJ flicks the key, the car beeps once and the doors unlock. It has the caged back seat. All that is missing are the cuffs.

Again I realize all eyes are on us as this unfolds. I am truly in such unknown territory that my mind can't decide whether to be scared or excited. It's safe to say, though, that for once, I am truly living in the moment. Not thinking about the past, not even worrying about what comes next. Just here and now, like my neighbour Mr. Jackson would say.

The officer opens the back door of the car and tugs at my arm. I guess I was just standing there because she lets out an extended exasperated breath, tilts her head slightly to the sky and whispers to an unnamed deity, "Give me strength." Then she puts that classic hand on my head like a priest blessing a parishioner and guides me into the back seat of the cruiser—into the cage.

I may be imagining it, but I think I hear clapping and even cheering coming from inside the school.

The drive to the police station is all too short. The whole town looks so different to me from the back seat of a police car. I make a point of giving eye contact to anyone we pass, but I don't see anyone I know. All the kids from school are still *in* school.

We stop at a red light and a woman walking her two little twins across the street scowls at me and that feels good. I want to push my face up against the window and maybe snarl or growl, but realize that would be too theatrical.

BJ talks on the car radio and says that we are on our way. I want her to use the word "suspect" or "perp" but it's just "we," like we are on a casual afternoon date.

I study the bun of BJ's hair, pressed up against the head-rest, and realize what really nice hair she has. It's a pity she keeps it wrapped up like that today, but then I guess a cop lady isn't supposed to look too glamorous on the job. Still, I can't help but wonder if she is dating anyone. Funny what goes through your head when sitting in the back of a police car.

"I want you to know, John Francis, I'm not enjoying this," she says. Maybe she had seen a half-smile on my face. "You're going to have to act more like you know you are in trouble and less like you're headed to a matinee at the movies."

"I'll try," I say, but I guess I still sound too cheerful.

"Try harder, dammit."

~

The police station in our town is half of a brick building shared with the public library. I'm sure this was a move that had economic implications, saving the taxpayers some money by some clever architect coming up with a municipal two-fer. Librarians and readers on one side, cops and robbers on the other. I'm more than a little familiar with the place, but this is my first time going in the north door instead of the south.

No one is around, so BJ just opens the back door of the car and I get out on my own. I finally have a chance to tuck my shirt in. Then I follow her dutifully (and with some more seriousness now) into the police station.

"Yvonne is still at lunch," a pale but otherwise handsome police officer says.

"Do we really have to do this?" BJ asks.

"Policy says yes. Better stick to the rules."

I am wondering what *this* referred to, but soon get distracted by seeing a box of donuts on a nearby desk.

Off to the side of the room is a short hallway with two cells. Jail cells. But only two of them. There are bars and everything and the smell is pretty awful. Pee and puke would be my guess. Only one cell is occupied.

"I'm not putting him in with Tommy," BJ insists. Tommy is apparently the guy sacked out on the metal bed in cell number one.

"Just put him in the other one," the pale cop says.

The door to cell number two is open and I walk in of my own accord. BJ looks at the door as it creaks open, and then back at her colleague with a questioning look. "Dave?"

Dave walks over and into the cell. He gives me the once-over. "Take off your shoelace," he orders.

It catches me off-guard, but then I remembered something—from one of my mom's movies, no doubt.

I dutifully sit on the bunk, breathing in the stink in the air and fumble with the left shoelace, threading it out of the holes in the running shoe my mom had bought me at Value Village. After a bit of struggling by me and eye-rolling on the part of BJ, I hand it to Officer Dave.

"Thanks," he says and I begin to undo the other one like a well-behaved criminal.

"No," Dave says, "I only need the one."

Dave and BJ are both standing outside the cell now and Dave was tying my cell door shut with my shoelace. "Lock's broke," he says. "Locksmith is on vacation. So this will have to do."

Nobody cracked a smile, but I suddenly feel considerably less of a criminal than I did moments before.

Dave gives me a look. "We're just waiting for the processing clerk to come back. We'll do up the paperwork, you'll get a court date and then you can go."

"We couldn't get hold of your mother," BJ said. "We may not be able to let you go unless she's here."

"My mother doesn't answer the phone. She tends to screen all the calls. I don't know what to say."

BJ looks exasperated again.

"I'm sorry," I added.

"Can I get you anything?" Dave asks, not at all sounding like someone who disdained my criminal behaviour. "Water?" I wonder why yet another cop is asking me if I'm thirsty.

"No thanks," I say politely.

But he must have noticed me looking longingly at the box of donuts sitting on his jumbled desk. "Want one?" he asks. "Plain or chocolate?"

"Are you kidding?"

He hands me just what the doctor ordered and seems to be studying me. "You know, people make fun of police officers and their presence at donut shops. It seems like such a cliché, but we put up with a lot of crap from the unrespecting public, so if a man in uniform wants to stop at Tim Hortons or Dunkin' Donuts for a little something to get through his shift, I say, let him have his sugar rush and get on with doing a difficult job."

"I couldn't agree more," I say, biting into a slightly-stale but still heavenly chocolate donut with cracked white glazing.

The two police officers turn away to let me enjoy my donut in peace.

Just about then Tommy wakes up in the cell next door. Maybe he smelled the donut and that did it. He sits up, scratches his face and then his balls, and yawns. His clothes are mightily rumpled and he looks like he hasn't shaved in a fair amount of time, but his salt-and-pepper beard looks like it isn't there to make him look manly. It's more the homeless, I-sleep-under-cardboard look.

At first, he just watches as I finish off the donut. This is probably not at all kind of me. He stares and says nothing, then coughs for a few minutes, spits something into the seatless toilet in his cell and says, "Hi, neighbour."

"Hi," I say back.

He studies the shoelace holding my cell door shut. "Hard-core, kid," he says. "What'd you do?"

"Stopped a fight," I say.

"Didn't know they could arrest you for that."

"It's a little complicated."

"Tell me about it." More coughing, more spitting.

By now I'm getting used to the smell of pee and puke and wondering why the ventilation isn't a bit better in a municipal building like this, but I figure that the person who deals with it is probably on vacation...or maybe it was intentional.

"Jesus," Tommy suddenly says. "My mouth tastes like the entire sewer system has run through there after every living soul in this damn town has flushed their toilets."

I don't like the sound of that. "What are *you* in for?" I decide not to comment on the fact that at least he has a real lock that works on his cell.

"Same old, same old."

I guess that it has something to do with drinking. *Drunk and disorderly* may be the term. I nod knowingly.

"I probably should clean up my act," Tommy says. "Hell, I'm forty-five years old and look at me."

He looks more like sixty and I think that he really *should* clean up his act. I suppose he spent more than just last night in the cell, but don't want to say anything negative. "How come they only have these two cells?" I ask, trying to keep up the chatter.

"They send the real criminals over to County. Usually it's just drunks and yahoos here."

"I guess that makes me a yahoo."

"Nah, you seem okay, kid. Probably just made a mistake. We all do from time to time."

I suddenly wonder if I might end up someday like my jail-house neighbour.

"Don't end up like me, kid," he says, as if reading my mind.

"What do you mean?"

"I let the booze get to me. Can't just have one drink. Got to finish the bottle and move on to the next, if you know what I mean."

"Ever think about going to the Recovery Room? I have a friend who goes there."

He laughs and coughs at the same time. "Right. Reverend Kevin, ole Shaky and the whole gang. Been there once, but they threw me out. The bastards said I couldn't drink there."

"Well, that's why they called it the Recovery Room. You're supposed to recover from whatever you're addicted to."

"Bunch of well-meaning, platitude-preaching do-good-ers."

"You should try it again."

"Maybe. But then, you're not the one with the craving for booze."

"I've got my issues," I say, trying to keep up my side of the discussion.

"What's your passion?" he now asks with great interest. I suppose he's expecting I'll say something really interesting, but I just tap on the old spare tire.

He seems truly disappointed. "Twinkies and donuts? Fried chicken and chips? Give me a break."

Him just saying those words makes me hungry. But not for long.

There is a sudden ruckus in the office at the end of the hall. A woman is shouting. Not just any woman. I recognize the voice of my mother.

"I demand to see my son!" she screams.

"Just calm down," I hear BJ say.

"Don't tell me to calm down," my mother snaps back, a phrase that I had heard many times in my life from the wo-man who had brought me into the world.

My mother has always been a highly-charged, emotional person and she thinks that anyone telling her to calm down is ignoring her very *modus operandi* of existence and has no right to express such an egregious thought.

"I'm okay, Mom. I'm back here," I shout.

In a split second she's standing at my door, Robin at her side. Robin had obviously gone to get her and here they are, the two most important women in my life.

"Let my son out of this god-damn animal cage!" Mom insists.

BJ casually walks towards her. "You can let him out yourself. The processing clerk is here now. We can do the paperwork and he can go."

My mom and Robin now see my shoelace, that Officer Donut Dave had tied just like he was tying his own shoe, with a large, loopy bow. Robin reaches past my mom, unties the lace, and the door swings open.

My mom gives me the first good hug I've had in a long time, and then I reach down to retrieve the lace from the floor.

"Nice getting to know ya," Tommy says. "Sorry we didn't get more chance to talk more. I bet we have a lot in common."

"Good luck," I tell him. "Don't forget about the Recovery Room."

The woman they called Yvonne fingerprints me, and I must have smudged it a couple of times because she keeps saying "Bugger" and then redoing it, gripping my fingers like they aren't even part of my body. With the sloppy job done, she stars filling out some form, an official looking paper that would have the court date.

Robin does a masterful job of keeping my mother from exploding all over the room, but Mom continues to glare at the police officers, especially Yvonne, whom she accuses of taking her own sweet time filling out the forms.

Dave offers me the last donut in the box as we are on the way out. It's a plain one but who am I to complain?

If it wasn't for the fact that someone had accused me of a

fairly serious crime, I would say it was one of the more interesting and enlightening afternoons of my life. But that is probably just the optimist in me trying to put a good spin on things.

Chapter Thirteen

My mom had driven to the police station in our twelve-year-old Ford. She didn't drive the car often because the registration and inspection had run out two or three years ago. We didn't have a lot of money so she believed she had a citizen's right to be negligent about some things. Since she had stopped smoking, she chewed a lot of gum and there was a considerable history of her car-driving, gum-chewing habits.

On our way home, I sit in the front seat and Robin is in the back.

Given the way things are going, I kind of wish my mom would let me drive. She is like a heated kettle about to boil and has road rage written all over her. I had taught myself how to drive a while back by watching instructional videos on YouTube. I'd sat in our car a few times and made a dry run or two, but don't have a license, of course. The only real driving I ever do is with Mr. Jackson's ancient Volvo station wagon with the little wiper blades on the headlights. Even then, he only lets me move the car backwards and forwards, up and down his short driveway.

My mom insists that I explain the whole sorry situation and Robin, reading me like a book as usual, offers to repeat the sorry tale in my stead. Robin always does have my back and I am content to sit there and watch the scenery: Burger King, Taco Bell, Apple Barrel, Harvey's, Arby's, KFC.

My mom is still fuming, and getting angrier by the minute as the story unfolds. She is popping one cube of Ice chewing gum in her mouth after another, despite the fact that I had warned her that the saliva produced by chewing gum erodes the enamel on your teeth.

She is simultaneously mouthing hushed curses at drivers in front of her whom she thinks are driving too slow. I know for sure she wants to ram our car into the rear bumper of the Honda Civic in front of us, driving *below* the speed limit. She is in that familiar mood where she wants to hit someone or break something.

As far back as I can remember, she only actually whacked me once. I was five at the time and had taken a kitchen knife and inserted it into the electric wall socket. She came running at me when she saw what I was up to and smacked me hard enough to knock me a few feet across the living room. Then she apologized and never did it again. And that was that.

She does a lot of screaming, but it is hardly ever directed at me. I can tell that she really wants to cut loose with a scream right here in the car, but I think she doesn't want to do it in front of Robin so she sucks in her breath, looks over at me with great concern and pulls the car into the parking lot of Wendy's.

It's like I've died and gone to heaven.

My mother orders a milkshake and I have a burger, some chili in a paper bowl and one of those baked potatoes I so love. We sit at a window table and allow Robin to criticize both the menu and the food we're eating while she herself drinks a cup of hot water that they offered to her for free.

She doesn't trust the coffee or the tea there. She says she'd read that neither was fair trade and that there were most likely herbicides in both. Even the water has its problems, though. It comes with a plastic lid, for starters.

"You know the damage these lids have done to the environment?" she says. It's a rhetorical question. "And city water, ugh. They take it out of the river, take the chemicals out and then put more chemicals back in. Ugh."

Her critique in no way interferes with my enjoyment of the food in front of me.

By the time Robin winds down on her ethical-eating sermon, I can see that the shake has settled my mom. Now she wants to discuss the legal territory ahead.

"So, Larkin's asshole father is the one who convinced the police to press charges even though it was his son who was beating up on Brady?"

"That appears to be the case," I say, licking the last bit of ketchup off the wrapper the burger had come in. "I don't think it was Larkin's idea. But his father is a big-shot lawyer."

"Do you remember the Dan Grogan case?" Robin asks my mom.

"The guy who swindled the Red Cross out of $100,000 and got off with a slap on the wrist?"

"Henry Kelsey was his lawyer. Got Grogan off on a technicality."

"And now he wants to see my son convicted?"

"Apparently so," Robin says. "And I don't trust the court or any judge to see the truth of the matter."

The look on my mom's face is a truly scary mix of fear and anger. "That's just not right," she says, crushing her milkshake cup even though it's still half full.

For my part, I just stare at the pattern left on my paper plate from the chives that had fallen like dead soldiers from the top of the sour cream that once crowned my split baked potato. It is really only starting to sink in that I might end up with some kind of serious punishment. Maybe get sent to one of those institutions for troublemaker teenagers, or even do time in an adult correctional facility. Things could get really ugly.

My mom has picked up her phone and is scrolling through screens. She now seems distracted, and that's a good thing.

Robin peeks over her shoulder to see what she is up to and scrunches up her face at what she sees.

Now my mom is all concentration. The fearful look she'd had a few minutes ago has vanished. The anger is still there, but a look of determination has joined it. I'd seen that look before, of course, and it usually leads to no good.

My mom sets the phone down on the table and gets up. "I gotta pee," she says. "I gotta pee before I explode," and she hustles off to the washroom. My mom is always like that, never taking a precautionary trip to the bathroom but waiting until some last-minute panic when her bladder is about to give out.

As soon as she is gone, Robin grabs that phone and holds it out for me to look at.

On the screen is a newspaper ad. It shows a tall, barrel-chested man in a suit, with expensive sunglasses on, standing in front of some kind of foreign, expensive, Jeep-like thing like you see in British movies. A Range Rover, I think it's called.

The caption reads, "Legal defence lawyer Henry Kelsey talks to reporters after winning successful suit against the school board for student playground injury."

Robin flips the screen and shows the listing on Yelp for lawyers that includes information for Kelsey, Gold, Green and Ragus. "Yes," she says.

"No," I say. "Please, Lord, no."

When Mom returns from the loo, she seems much calmer, now that she's relieved her bladder. She clears the clutter from our table like a good mother would and dumps wrappers and cups into the trash and even wipes a few chives and crumbs from the table.

"Enough of this," she says in what I know to be her deceptively-calm fashion. "Let's get going." She grabs her phone and takes one last look at the Yelp screen.

Robin slides into the back seat again and I ride shotgun. My mom turns on the radio with the cracked speaker to an all-news channel but then punches through a few more radio stations, making guttural noises at the rap music, and finally locating an oldies station playing Bruce Springsteen's "Born to Run." She turns it up until the speaker rattles, humming along like we were all off on a family picnic to the lake or something.

We are not on our way home, nor, however, to the lake. Mom is on a mission.

"I think we should just cool off for a bit," I say. "Don't you think that's a good idea, Mom? Just go home. Robin and I will have some orange juice and I'll make you one of those drinks you like—what do you call it, a screwdriver?"

She waves a hand in the air. "John Francis, you know I gave up drinking when I stopped smoking."

"Well, then, me and Robin will make you a nice cup of tea."

"A cup of tea just won't do it right now," she says.

She has that look in her eyes. Whatever it is she has in mind, I know there is no stopping her.

"I'm glad you're with us, Robin," she says as Bruce races off on his motorcycle with his girl on the back and the wind in their hair. "We're in this together, right?"

"Hell, yeah," Robin says.

But when I look at her, she just shrugs.

"You're a good kid," she tells Robin. "You stand up for what you believe in. Somebody's gotta do that."

"There's a lot of injustice in the world," Robin admits, one of her favourite mantras.

I know that whatever was going to happen, it isn't going to be good. I can't count the number of times I've tried to divert my own sweet mother from some manic path she got herself on.

She is driving better now, though, not cursing at other drivers nearly as much and, as she turns off the radio, says to the windshield, "God, I could use a smoke."

Then, leaning toward me, "John F, see if I have more gum in the glove compartment."

Fortunately, she does. I pop out four of those little green

cubes and hand them to her.

"That's better," she says, her mouth stuffed with the gum and her teeth working overtime.

We are headed downtown, to the business district where we almost never go. Despite the fact that I figure we are driving into disaster, I am trying to content myself with the thought that I am at least sitting in the family automobile with the two most important women in my life. My mom and me are inseparable no matter how bad things get, and Robin is as loyal a friend as anyone could have. The glass is more than half full.

And then we pull into the parking lot of a three-storey brick edifice called The Professional Building. "Professional, my arse," my mom says.

She looks like she is ready to spit the gum out. It never lasts very long for her and she claims that the corporations who sell chewing gum have reduced the quality of the product over the years to something shameful.

I know her electric window is busted, so I hit the button so mine opens, and lean back. Without missing a beat, she spits her wad across in front of me and out into the parking lot.

I know Robin would be wanting to say something about the environmental impact of people like my mom recklessly spitting gum. But she doe not.

We are circling the parking lot now, driving up and down the aisles, my mom craning her neck, looking at each vehicle. Robin and I both know what she is looking for. The parking lot is not quite half full of cars and there is no one walking.

We were on the last aisle, furthest from the building, when we all spot the only Range Rover in the parking lot—shiny, spanking-new, sitting beneath the only tree at the edge of the lot.

"He parked it in the shade, I see," Mom says.

Robin and I know exactly who "he" is.

"Oh shit," I say. "Please, can't we just go home?"

My mom stops the car and puts it in park. She leaves the engine running but hits the button to open the trunk.

"This will only take a minute," she says, and with that she is out of the car and running to the back.

"Damn," I say, getting out as quickly as I can to stop her. In another life, my mother must have been a warrior or Babe Ruth maybe or just an ordinary jilted lover in a bad country song, because she moves with practised power, grace and precision.

The Louisville Slugger is now out of the car. Her feet barely touch the pavement as she approaches the automotive victim and swings the bat.

One, two, three, four, five. Tail lights, headlights, windshield.

The bat bounces off the windshield once, leaving only a small circle of cracked glass. It takes two more swings, evoking the spirit of the Babe himself, before the safety glass goes concave and then shatters into a thousand shiny little cubes and rains down on the interior of the fancy car.

My mom looks to the heavens and starts back our way, only to have second thoughts and return to the car. She delivers another home run to the driver's-side door, punching it in and then setting off the air bag, that blows some kind of white powder in a dramatic puff out through the gaping hole that had once been a windshield.

Oddly enough, it is only then that the car alarm goes off.

Robin had stayed in the car. I am standing on the sidewalk not knowing what to do or say when Mom breezes past me. "Drive," she says. "You need to drive. I can't."

She walks to the back of our car, throws the bat into the trunk, and gets in the front passenger seat. "Drive, please," she insists. "Now."

I get into the car and put it in gear. It is probably the most cautious, slow getaway in the history of criminal activity as I drive us out of there. My mom sits upright, staring straight ahead, shaking.

No one says a word as we crawl through the town traffic, me stopping at red lights a bit too early and watching for police cars, thinking, *If they arrest us now, maybe Mom and me could share a cell.*

Chapter Fourteen

Robin sits silently in the back as I drive us home. I think she's both impressed and a little scared at the same time. Me, I keep listening for sirens and looking in my rear-view mirror.

I can hear Mr. Jackson's low monotone voice in my head reminding me, *When things get really rough, go deep inside and find your inner peace. It will give you strength.* But it takes all my wits to keep my hands on the wheel, keep the old Ford on the correct side of the road and get us all home in one piece.

I find it nearly impossible to believe that no one saw my mother's Range Rover home run, but we arrive home unimpeded and intact. Once home, I help my mom into the house, where she takes a prescribed Valium.

Robin doesn't like to watch her swallowing the pill and bows out. "I'm going home to check on how much rain forest has been destroyed today," she says.

I want to hug her for being there with us, but resist.

Mom then insists I binge-watch reruns of *Seinfeld* with her. She offers to make popcorn and nachos, so who was I to speak otherwise?

There are no knocks at the door, no phone calls from the

police. Nothing.

I give up on TV after a bit, once I'd had my fill of TV snacks, and go into my room to do my homework. Yes, in the midst of all the turmoil, it actually feels good to be doing homework in my quiet bedroom.

That is, until my mom takes a break from laughing at Jerry, Elaine, George and Kramer and yells, "John Francis, quick, get in here."

When I get into the room, there's Henry Kelsey on TV, standing by his car with the smashed-in windshield. Around here, he is a somewhat familiar face on TV. Most everyone knows who he is because of those locally-famous criminal trials, even a couple of murder ones where most of us in the community believed the accused to be guilty. Kelsey is famous for his invocation of legal technicalities and police misconduct. He is as unlikable as a man could get in this day and age but seems to garner praise from the media and from local politicians who claim to be his friends.

So, as my mom sits there with her jaw dropped and a can of Mountain Dew halfway to her lips, here is Henry Kelsey, standing by his multiply damaged car and asking the viewing audience for sympathy. "So I'm just leaving the office and I come out here and look at what I find. Another indication of the rise of lawlessness in this town. An indication that the police are not doing their job of protecting the property of the good citizens who live here. This senseless destruction of private property has got to stop."

"Who do you think did this?" a woman reporter asks.

"I think it's personal," he says. "I've been serving this community with my legal advocacy for ten years now and it comes with a price. When you work for the common good of the people, there are always naysayers who spark enmity and want to destroy those of us who work day in and day out in the name of justice and peace." This from the man who defends wife-beaters and murderers.

"Do you have insurance?" another reporter asks.

"Insurance is irrelevant," Mr. Kelsey nearly shouts, putting his hand on the dented driver's door and looking like he is doing only half his job of containing the Vesuvian rage that must be building up inside him. He half-turns and looks straight at the camera. "If someone thinks they can do a heinous crime like this and get away with it, I want to tell them right now they are wrong." Then suddenly *they* changes to *he*. "Whoever *he* is," Kelsey says, moving in a bit too close to the camera, forcing the cameramen to refocus, "I want him to know, I'll track him down and bring the full extent of the law to bear."

The camera shifts to the young reporter, who has taken a few steps back. Blinking, she says, "Over to you, Jeff."

And that is that.

A half-smile comes upon my mother's face. "He thinks it was a man," she says triumphantly. "He thinks it's someone who wants to get back at him for setting free a thief or a blackmailer."

"Or a murderer," I add, hoping she is right, that it is unlikely Kelsey would think there is any connection between the car damage and his own son's locker room scuffle with a fellow schoolboy.

My mother takes a sip from the can of Mountain Dew, sets it on the table, turns off the TV and gives me two thumbs up.

I go back to my room to finish my homework, but before I go to bed, I loiter on social media for a bit, only to discover that the video of the now infamous locker room brawl has been viewed by (gulp) thousands and had been reposted endless times. The comments posted range from ridiculous to outrageous to, well, just about everything under the sun. Many are hideously insulting about me personally, which is to be expected, I suppose. It's amazing how anonymity brings out the worst in time-wasters on the infernal internet.

I note a few new, clever, but insulting terms for a young man like myself that I have to look up on Urban Dictionary. Mostly, there are less inventive insults all too familiar to a person like me. Sticks and stones really. That's the way I try to take it.

But on the flip side, I note comments coming from as far away as England, the Czech Republic and even Japan giving me kudos. "He must have deserved it," says an Australian. "Who is this dude?" asks a girl from Minnesota. I don't know if it's a good or bad thing or that she called me "dude", so I decide that it's positive, right?

And, as I lie on my bed, hoping to fall into a deep sleep, it occurs to me that I might actually be someone's hero. Even if it is only one girl in Minnesota, a girl I will never meet.

Of course, this would mean I'd have to revamp my number one rule that there are no heroes in the kingdom of grilled cheese sandwiches. But probably not yet.

~

The court date is a week away. At breakfast my mother tells me we probably have to get a lawyer, "one without a smashed windshield," she adds, unable to hide a guilty smile as she pours her coffee. "We have no money, so we'll have to use the public defender."

I don't exactly know what that is, but I guess it must be a lawyer you don't have to pay. Probably some inexperienced young person straight out of one of those expensive private law schools for dummies.

I guess I should be scared, fearful for my future, but, oddly, I'm not. I feel like a new, completely unlikely and unique version of the heroic male. A twenty-first-century knight. A weighty warrior and soon-to-be-famous fighter. Defender of the little guy (Brady). The unknown wide warrior admired by young women (well, at least one young woman, maybe) in Minnesota.

Or not. Anyway, time to go to school and see what yet another Memorial High School day will be like.

I decide to walk to school, if only to clear my head and try to do some good, old-fashioned, bipedal cogitation. Many great thinkers claimed that walking and thinking went hand in hand, although I can't remember their names.

It's a decent spring morning and I notice a lot of birds in the trees and new shoots of green everywhere. I am still worrying about my mom and her temper, her streak of anger, her desire to fight back at a world she sees as uncaring and hostile. She is already on thin ice at her job at the beauty supply store. It really isn't her ideal job, but she's been fired so many times she's lucky that an old friend had hired her, even if it was only part-time.

I know I should be worrying about my future, but I have what the Japanese (did I mention I have at least one fan in that far-off nation?) refer to as a *satori* moment. An inexplicable, brief, but definable feeling of well-being. What Mr. Jackson would probably refer to as feeling "at one with the world."

Why this would happen to a hapless boy like me while walking to school—where kids would continue to stare at and taunt me—is hard to say. But it probably has something to do with walking.

Why hadn't I realized this before? Wanna fix your head? Take a longish walk. That's what your ancestors did in the plains of Africa 10,000 years ago. Clearly, we should never have fooled around with motor-assisted modes of transportation.

All too soon, I arrive at the front of the school, where I can watch all the other, less-adventurous students getting off the yellow buses. I am still one of them, but something within me has changed. I know that, for good or bad, I have moved on from being ordinary.

Maybe everyone feels that way at some point in their lives. But I had not felt special at any other time up until this point. The now-legendary (in my head) locker room intervention. Video fame—international at that. Charged with a crime. Time in jail (well, a short time with the door held in place with my own shoelace). More potential persecution. Online Minnesota sweetheart. *Satori* bird-singing morning. What a great life. I want so badly to share this conclusion, this slightly (or grossly) illogical morning euphoric epiphany, with my good friend, Robin.

But no luck. Robin is not around. And Mr. Battle is waiting for me. "Mr. Morgan is back from his conference. He wants to see you right away."

It doesn't exactly destroy the moment. My inner voice, the one that often said things highly irrational but braces me for bad things to come, prompts me with the notion that *This is just another step along the way in the great adventure.*

I know that sounds like a load of crap, but these had turned into the most extraordinary times, and I was learning day by day that almost anything could happen. Even a meeting with Mr. Morgan.

I say that because Dr. Mantel Morgan is hardly ever seen at school. He is known almost exclusively as Dr. Morgan. That's what everyone is supposed to call him. He has a Ph.D. in education and he attends a great number of teacher/ administrator conferences, where he gives a great number of apparently-inspiring speeches on the future of education.

He is a bit of an enigma around the school, though, since he is here so rarely. He has four vice principals because we are a big school so Dr. Morgan rarely has to deal with an actual, live, human student.

Clearly, he prefers it that way, sitting in his sumptuous and isolated office if he is there at all, where he does something or other to keep the school running like clockwork. Or maybe he just writes speeches and learned papers on the future of education. No one really knows.

I suppose he bosses around the VPs and makes them do the heavy lifting. He accepts invitations to those famous conferences where there are undoubtedly cocktail gatherings afterwards with lofty administrators like him who probably let their hair down after a couple of martinis. Who knows?

Dr. Morgan also appears in the local newspapers at least once annually for receiving an honorary doctorate (what is that, anyway?), some kind of Principal of the Year award from an obscure organization of sycophants, or having his picture taken with a former astronaut, a Nobel Prize laureate, a politician running for the highest office in the land or a high-up corporate representative from Pepsi, Google, Apple, Amazon, Staples or Samsung trying to land a really lucrative educational deal at Memorial High.

Once in a blue moon, Dr. Morgan announces an assembly and we all file into the auditorium donated by Pepsi Cola. We are grateful to be released from whatever class was interrupted, but mostly sit slack-jawed and mystified by whatever it is Morgan the Man is speaking about. I'd tried on numerous occasions to make sense of his speeches since I like his big words and big ideas and, long after every other student in the Pepsi Hall has gone to sleep or slunk off mentally to distant lands, I analyze what he'd actually said with his elevated vocabulary and it always comes down to some very simple things:

Do your work
Don't disturb the status quo
Listen to your teachers
Do more work
Take final exams seriously

Be a team player
Don't rock the boat (see above)

"We don't need another hero," he said more than once, drawing my attention to that word. "We just need hard workers."

The last line is his trademark conclusion to a long-winded oration. I think he borrowed it from a song or a Spider-man movie, but I may have been the only one to notice.

In the school office, I go past two secretaries and two outer doors to where Mr. B taps on the solid, mahogany door of Dr. Morgan's inner sanctum.

"Come in," orders the voice.

Dr. Morgan is impeccably dressed, as always. He is about forty, with a well-trimmed beard, an immaculate white shirt and a blue tie. And a suit straight out of a James Bond movie. He nods to Mr. B, and the VP bows slightly as he eases himself backwards out the door without a word.

There is one chair—a solid, wooden one with a broad seat, as it turns out— in front of the desk.

I know that I am still in trouble, and I also know that Dr. Morgan likes to hear himself talk, so I decide to play it fairly mute and not even ask for my student advocate to be present on my behalf. Robin has already done enough to help me. The morning walk told me I need to face some things on my own without the aid of a tall, loyal, tattooed vegan friend or a bat-wielding mother.

"John Francis, is it?" he begins.

I nodded, taking Mr. Battle's lead of non-vocalization.

"John Francis, you know I like to get to know each and

every student in this school," he says, looking partially my way but more focused on some spot on the wall high over my head.

The statement is a bit of a yarn. Almost no one ever has an audience with him unless it involves a photo op with a student who has rescued twin boys from drowning in a river or come up with a cure for cancer.

"But I've never had a chance to get to know you, first-hand."

He isn't really looking for an explanation, so I remain po-litely silent, smiling beatifically as I had practised before the mirror at home.

"I assume this is because you've never been in trouble, never given this fine institution any grief or shown any ill will against another student." And, of course, he is right on all those counts, obviously putting his graduate degree and assortment of honorary doctorates to good cerebral use in the conversation.

"But now we have this incident," he says, his voice chan-ging considerably and his eyes dropping from above to look me squarely in the eyes. "Mr. Battle has explained to me what you told him about the extenuating circumstances and, while we have no tangible evidence that you are telling the truth, I will entertain your side of the story as a valid possibility."

"Thank you," I say, finally adding a small smidgen of my-self to the one-sided conversation.

"I myself spoke to Brady Roberts and he said nothing of the sort happened."

"I know. I'm not surprised. That's the way these things go

sometimes."

The principal is not pleased with my response. "That's how you see it? *These things*?"

I know it would be fairly pointless to try to explain further. Besides, I am really tired of telling the whole story and know I'd do a poor job of it, anyway. Silence, if not actually golden, is a worthy bit of currency in a pinch.

"You are aware that Larkin's father has filed serious complaints against you, but what you don't know is that he is suing the school board, and our school in particular, for a fairly large sum of money."

"He can do that?" I blurt out.

"He can and he has. And that's why I've called you in here today for this little *tête à tête*."

The French throws me off. I knew *tête* is some part of the human body, but not sure which part. Ankle, toe, chest, neck? Ah, yes, it comes to me: head. A head-to-head meeting of minds.

"I didn't bring you in here to lecture you on why what you did was wrong. And I've seen the evidence. Who hasn't? I'll let the legal authorities deal with that. But, unfortunately for me"—he puts considerable inflection on the word *me* —"it's now my problem as well. Mr. Kelsey is not likely to back off unless we offer up something tangible."

I am thinking of something biblical. My head on a platter? Who was that? John the Baptist, I think. John the Baptist and John Francis. We'd have something in common.

"We could metaphorically slap you on the wrist," he continues, adjusting his tie and then stroking his facial hair. "But the optics would not be good. And I've ruled out a mere suspension. Not enough."

My inexplicable morning euphoria has slipped out through the thin crack under the mahogany door.

"I don't like any form of punishment that will deter a single student from potential academic success, you know that?"

It isn't really much of a question. No one knows much of anything about Dr. Morgan. But it sounds ominous to my ears.

"So we've decided to let you go."

What the hell does that mean? I'm not being fired from a job. This is high school, for Chrissakes.

"You're letting me go?"

"We'll have to terminate your association with Memorial. Make an example of you so others don't follow your lead."

My head is spinning now and I really don't understand what he is saying. "I've never thought of myself as much of a role model for my peers," I say. "But am I being expelled?"

"Not at all. We don't use that word these days. You simply won't be permitted to come to school anymore."

"So what then? I do home schooling?"

"No, we couldn't sanction that. You'll be able to seek a private education to finish high school and we'll be more than accommodating to whomever takes you in. We'll provide your academic records but, beyond that, you will no longer be associated in any way with Memorial High."

Stunned silence now on my part. Not the golden kind at all. Instead, a deep-in-the-pit-of-a-collapsed-mine kind of dark and deadly silence.

Dr. Morgan stands up now, tugs at his suit jacket like

James Bond would have done. "I want to thank you for coming in and for not making this any harder than it needed to be. As you can understand, I've found this whole affair most upsetting. It was more than a little taxing and I had to come home early from my conference to handle this personally. It didn't seem fair to ask any of my colleagues to do this. I wish you all the best."

I guess he pushed some kind of button for the school security guard who must have been waiting right outside the door. He promptly walks in and stands there.

"Please take John Francis to his hall locker, allow him to pick up his personal belongings, and then escort him off school property. I don't think he'll give you a hard time."

And then, looking at me: "Will you, John Francis?"

And that's how I get kicked out of school.

Chapter Fifteen

The security guy is a kind of rent-a-cop, a burly Memorial graduate named Oakley who had played a good game of football in high school but peaked early in his career, I guess, and ended up as a high-school daily security guard. He sometimes can be seen breaking into kids' lockers by smashing a personal combination lock off with a heavy ball peen hammer and then rummaging around for drugs or weapons. He has a good personality, though, and like me, lets insults slip off him like water off a duck's back.

I'm not about to give ole Oakley a hard time. Personally, I think he is confused sometimes, like he'd been hit too hard in the head during dozens of tackles in high school sports.

I myself, believe it or not, had dabbled with the idea of playing high school football. And it had been Oakley, a few years older and highly-regarded by the school sports fans, who had said I should try out for the team. If I worked it right, he said, I could use my weight as an advantage as a guard or something. More than once, I'd been compared to an immovable object.

"Let's do the locker thing," Oakley now says.

"You won't need the hammer," I say.

"I know that. I left it in my office."

Oakley's office is more like a spare janitor's closet, but he seems proud of it. "You should have gone out for football," he says. "I really miss it. You could have been one hell of a tackle."

"But now this?"

"Yeah, this. Sucks to be you."

"Sometimes it does. Sometimes it doesn't."

Truth is, I have grown weary of worrying about me. I am more worried about my mom. The grief I am causing her from the locker room incident, the baseball bat thing, and now this could push her over the edge. Until recently, that Louisville Slugger had just been a symbol of power. Now it has moved right out of the metaphorical realm and into real life.

I make a mental note to hide that bat when I get home. Maybe the sharper of the kitchen knives as well. Mom is a bit too jumpy now, and I'd hate to see her take a stab at the postman or a Jehovah's Witness.

"Oakley, what do you think I should do?" I know that Oakley would have heard various versions of what happened—some from the kids, some from the administration.

"Fuck knows. I was in plenty of punch-ups when I was in football. It was expected in those days. Bloody a nose or two. Crack a rib. All part of growing up. Now, it's all different."

"'Optics', Morgan called it. What did he mean?"

"It's all about how things look—how they appear. You took the crap out of Pretty Boy and it looks bad so you get the bum's rush."

"I overdid it with the head thing."

"I, too, thought that was over the top. I mean, you had him slammed up against the locker. Point made."

"I don't know what got into me."

"Shit happens. Listen, I'm sorry it had to happen to you."

We're at my locker now. I pull out my book bag and start to put a couple of textbooks in.

"Uh oh," Oakley says. "School property. You better leave them."

"That's right. I've been terminated. I'm not coming back."

It is really just beginning to sink in. And, strange to say, I think this exile from my high school seems more real than the criminal charges. Really. *I'm not coming back to school.* The end of my world as I knew it.

Oakley sees the look of despair on my face. Am I really about to cry? "Fuck this," he says, exhaling loudly. "You wanna sit in my office and pull yourself together?"

"Yeah, I do. I don't want to go home right now."

"Understood. C'mon."

I reach inside my locker for two paperbacks I had kept stashed there—my own books. A biography of Albert Einstein and an old, dog-eared copy of *The Catcher in the Rye.*

Oakley looks a little puzzled.

"They're mine, not the school board's. Don't worry. Okay if I just read there for a little bit?"

"Read?"

"Yeah, reading in school. One more time for old times' sake."

Oakley blows some air out of his mouth that makes his lips flap together the way you do when you're a really little rug rat. "Well, they are right about you, JFC. You are a weird one. But hell, yes, if you want to read, go for it. Fill your boots. But then later I'll have to sneak you out the back way into the bus parking lot, or I'll be in deep diaper drippings."

"Thanks, Oakley."

"Just taking one for the team."

So he leads me to his little windowless office, sits me at his pint-size desk, tells me not to mess with his scissors, stapler or computer. "Look, you can stay here, but don't rock the boat. And I'm doing this because I like you and because I know you would have made a kick-ass football player. Read your damn book and, when I come back, I'll escort you out without anyone seeing."

"Thanks, dude."

"You got shit coming your way, little buddy, so you deserve a bit of a break."

I don't think anyone has called me "little" for a very long time.

Its true: wanting to read a book at a time like this must seem like a pretty bizarre thing. Reading a good book has always steadied my nerves and mentally and physically made me feel better. Just like walking this morning.

Wow. Maybe that's it. Whatever the future could bring, if I could still read and walk, I'd be okay. Maybe they'd let me do that in the slammer—or the correction facility, as I think it is called. An interesting word, correction: making something wrong into something right.

My eyes go from the top of the page of the Einstein bio book to the bottom but I can't remember much of what I just read. Something about a patent office, some theory about time and that young Albert had proposed some laughable theory (at least to those around him) that nothing, absolutely nothing at all, happens at the *exact* same time. No such thing.

Too much for me right then.

Next, I start rereading Salinger and take on the pain of Holden Caulfield one more time to replace my own fears and worries.

Then there's a knock at the door.

Shit.

When I don't answer, it opens. Robin has found me. She sees me at the desk in a pool of light, reading, and slips quietly in with the door barely opened more than a few inches.

But then Lawrence Battle is right behind her. He pushes himself in, gently closes the door and suddenly there's a crowd in the little space.

"Oakley told me you were here," Mr. Battle says. "Dr. Morgan knows you haven't left the building. If he finds you here, Oakley will probably lose his job, but Morgan will probably also call the police to have you removed."

I could see the headlines now. "Memorial Student Escorted From School For Reading J.D. Salinger In A Closet."

"He's right," Robin says. "We got to get you out of here now."

So much for my brief asylum in the arms of literature. I am beginning to think that maybe this is just the beginning of my life on the run. Maybe prison isn't in the offing, after all. Maybe I'd just flee prosecution. Create that new identity, find a job, live in a new town. Change the colour of my hair.

No. Shit. I can't see it. I actually more or less like who I am. And, besides, I can't abandon my mom.

I think Mr. Battle is looking around the small room to see if there was some kind of coat or something to cover me up in. But there is nothing big enough to do the job.

He shrugs. "I know where all the cameras are. We'll have to dodge them, but we gotta go now. Classes change in eight minutes. Kids will notice. Gotta skedaddle: leave your books."

So I leave my books. Albert and Holden, sorry, pals. Man on the run.

There is a narrow hallway next to the cafeteria that leads to the rear lot where buses park. Mr. Battle is confident that someone would have disabled the security cam for this area by this time of day. It was a pretty regular thing.

The hallway smelled of weed and, as we enter, a guy and girl tuck their heads down and run for the outside door. They are gone before we got there, and soon we are in the clear.

Robin nods. Mr. Battle retreats inside.

We slip between the tightly-parked buses and across a stretch of grass until we are into the patch of woods behind the school. Smoker's Paradise, as some call it.

Robin is nimble on her feet and I am not. I have to stop to catch my breath once we are completely in the shelter of the trees.

There is litter everywhere. Candy bar wrappers, cigarette packs, beer cans. High school kids are not kind to Mother Nature.

I guess I look pretty pathetic as I flop down on a fallen

maple tree, breathing heavily.

"What do you want to do?" Robin asks. "I've got some money saved. If you want, we can run. Just go away."

"I thought about that," I say. "Can't do it. You don't need to run. And I gotta stay with my mom."

"Your mother's crazy."

"I know. Everyone knows. What's she gonna do if I'm gone?"

Chapter Sixteen

Robin walks me to my door, and I feel I have to give her a hug. I don't do that very often. Robin has some kind of issue with physical contact even when it is meant to be a sign of affection.

She has been my friend for a very long time, but there is a lot about her I don't understand. Aside from me, she really doesn't have any friends. She acts aloof and opinionated and has a look that most kids just read as *Stay back. Keep away.*

Sometimes I ask her questions that she finds too personal and she just says, "I don't want to talk about it." Sometimes, if I try too hard, she shuts down. Sometimes she just walks away. So I stopped asking about the drug use, her own difficulties at home or even her future. She refuses to talk about her future.

We look odd together and people make fun of us. We know what they are thinking, but we got over that long ago.

I once asked Robin outright if she was into guys or girls, and her answer was simply, "Neither." I could have pried more. I really wanted to understand that, but again I got, "I don't want to talk about it."

Not that I have much going in terms of relationships. I

mean, I absolutely like girls, but it's not like I'd have much of a shot at any one I know for a girlfriend. Maybe someday I'll hook up with a girl on an online dating site. But now is not the time.

I walk into the house, still thinking about how Robin had gone kind of stiff when I tried to hug her. I was also thinking about what she said about me taking charge. Events are rolling over me and I am just letting things happen. But isn't that the way my life has always gone?

"Mom, I'm home," I say. She always wants me to announce myself because sometimes I scare her accidentally. She is pretty jumpy, my mom. Afraid of intruders. Ready to pounce at the slightest noise. I always have to be careful.

"John Francis, come see who's here," she shouts from the kitchen.

My mom had a visitor? Really?

When I walk into the kitchen, I nearly drop to the floor.

It's my father.

"He's come home," my mom says. And she says it with her happy voice. The one I almost never hear. It is like I just dropped into that alternate universe.

"John Francis," my dad says. "You've grown."

"Dad? What's up?" is all I can muster.

"I came to help."

"You came home to help me?"

"Yes. I'm a lawyer, remember?"

Well, I remember that he was some kind of tax lawyer with a big firm. He never spoke about his work; he always let on that he had one of the most boring jobs in the world. I am not sure how a tax lawyer can help me.

"I guess," I say.

"I've been trying to explain things to your mother," he says. "I was deeply depressed when I left here. My job. My life. I thought I needed to get away and figure out who I really was and what I needed to do with my life."

This doesn't sound like much of an explanation or an apology to me. "You've been gone a long time," I say. "Aside from a birthday and a Christmas card, we haven't even heard from you."

Every year when those cards arrived, my mother would scream at the wall and tear them into little pieces. But now she is sitting at the kitchen table with my loser father, who has just parachuted back into our lives. And she seems strangely pleased by this turn of events.

"I had to work some things out," he says. What a jerk.

"And how did that go?"

"It wasn't easy. Nothing justifies what I did. I just had to do it."

I don't really want to hear it. In fact, I don't really want this renegade runaway father back in my life.

"It was like mental illness," my mother adds. Weird that she would come to his defence.

"Bullshit," I say.

"I understand that I don't deserve to be forgiven. I don't even deserve to be your father. But I saw that video. Somebody showed it to me on their phone in a bar. And I said, 'That's my son,' and something snapped inside me. I realized I'd been running away all my life. Running scared. And when I watched it again, I realized you were doing the thing I'd never had the courage to do. You were standing up for yourself. You were tired of taking shit from people."

Well, that wasn't exactly it, but I realize my father, that unreliable man who had been nearly invisible even when he lived with us, has just opened up to me more than he'd done the whole time he'd lived here.

"So, like, we're just supposed to take you back into our lives like nothing happened?"

"No," he says assertively. "I'm going to have to earn the respect of you and your mother. I'll do whatever it takes."

"I told your father about the car incident," my mom says.

I look at my father and he shrugs.

We are seeing each other in that instant, I mean looking at each other eye to eye, something we had never ever done. And it suddenly occurs to me how much we look alike. He is a bit chunky around the neck and jowls, like me. His shoulders have that rounded look, like mine. But even more than that, we have the same nose, the same eyes, the same slightly-moist, sweaty forehead. And it suddenly occurs to me—like a lightning bolt out of the blue—that I actually do have a father. I have a fairly messed up, deadbeat dad of a father who bolted from our lives years ago. And now he is back.

Is it possible to both love and hate someone at the exact same time? I didn't know the answer to that up until this very minute.

"Welcome home, Dad," I say sarcastically. "You loser. Disappear again and I'll track you down and cut your balls off."

I have no idea where that came from. None whatsoever.

"That's my boy," he says, taking my mother's hand in his own and giving it a squeeze.

Chapter Seventeen

So there's this funny "take charge" theme to the day. In fact, everything is rather strange as the alternate universe has somehow adopted me into it. And I guess I was so very willing to be adopted.

My mother looks at the clock. "Why don't you two boys get to know each other all over and I'll make us a nice dinner."

No, that couldn't possibly be my mother speaking. I'd never heard that tone or that combination of words in years.

She walks towards the back door and puts the Louisville Slugger into the hallway closet. "How about I make us spaghetti?"

When my mother "makes spaghetti," she usually means opening up a can of Chef Boyardee and throwing it into a pot until it burns. I usually eat a whole can by myself, as you can imagine. My mother buys it by the case at the discount market (along with the economy size—five pounds—of cheddar cheese).

"Not just spaghetti," she says, correcting herself from down the hall. "Angel hair pasta. *Capelli d'angelo.*"

She walks towards us wielding the box of pasta like a

sports trophy. I crack a big smile and the anger I had felt towards my parachuting father disappears into thin air.

When she returns to the kitchen she has a bottle of wine. Uh oh.

My father studies the bottle. It's cheap wine, I know that. And she had opened it maybe a year ago. She had decided to take up drinking again at one point to relieve her anxiety, but didn't get farther than the first glass. "Not my cup of tea," she had declared and put it away in the closet.

Now it's on the table as a form of a homecoming celebration for the wandering tax lawyer. I think that red wine opened and then recorked and relegated to the cracker closet for twelve months must not taste very good, but then what do I know about wine?

Three mismatched small jelly jars are set upon the table. She pours something like a tablespoonful in each. "What is it people say at a time like this? Shalom?"

My father doesn't correct her. I was pretty sure shalom is Hebrew for "peace" but that seems more appropriate than "salut" or "cheers" or "down the hatch."

"Shalom," he repeats as we lift our jelly jars and slug back the purply liquid that tastes incredibly putrid. Since my mom had given up cigarettes and booze, we'd never been much of a drinking family and, from the looks on my parents' faces, this was unlikely to change.

"I'm gonna slice some onions," she says. "You boys continue to catch up and I'll listen in."

I'd never seen my mother slice an onion in my life. I was always worried when she hauled out that big knife. Sometimes, I'd hide it if she was acting really crazy. You just never knew. But this is different.

My father leans in towards me. "What I want to know first, John Francis, is if you are okay."

"Okay is relative," I answer ambiguously. "Physically, I feel okay, aside from being a little hungry, but Mom should take care of that shortly. Mentally, I'm a bit dazed. I seem to have gotten myself into a jam and it's escalated all on its own. Today, I was terminated at school. You know, like expelled. If I can't go to Memorial, what am I going to do?"

"Don't worry about that. Your mother and I will figure something out. There's always private school."

"But that takes money."

"Money is not an issue," he responds.

Money had *always* been an issue, before he left and more so after. Now my father is either delusional or he'd won the lottery. I'm hoping it's the latter.

"I may even get locked up somewhere."

"I won't let that happen."

"You know who the father is of the kid I slammed?"

"Kelsey, I know. Everyone knows him. He probably knows the judge. I bet the judge even owes him a favour. But that's neither here nor there. Men like Kelsey need to be knocked down a notch or two."

"And you think you can do that?"

"I know I can do that," he says, pouring another slug of the vile liquid into his jar and knocking it back like a shot of whiskey.

My mother starts crying at this point. "Don't worry about me. It's the onions."

"You should have sliced them under water," I tell her. "We

learned that in science class."

"My son, the genius," she says, and laughs as the tears flow. It's a good laugh, like we are all sharing an innocuous joke.

My father—I can't call him Dad with real sincerity just yet—goes over to my mother. He looks like he's going to hug her, but then he just kind of tentatively caresses the back of her neck.

She wipes the tears away on her sleeve and smiles in a way I had not seen in years. She leans into his touch on her neck. I look away, not ready to play Happy Family.

My father says, "Look, I'd like to tell you both my story, if that's okay. I'm not trying to absolve myself of anything. I just think you have the right to know why I was so useless to you both."

My mom nods and blows her nose on the dish towel.

I say, "Sure." I figure we'd hear a load of bull, but I am curious all the same.

"Okay. I'll try to keep it short." He rubs his hand over his mouth like he's nervous, as he damn well should be.

My father was a total shit. Before he left, he made me feel like I was never good enough. He did the same thing to my mother. At school, my insecurity showed so I had my tormentors. The names changed through the years but the rules of the game were the same.

"I never had a chance to form my own identity," he begins, "except as the kid who is never good enough, the one you can make fun of when you need a good laugh, the kid who looked scared all the time. Was scared all the time. The only thing I was good at was math. I loved numbers. I could hide in numbers."

"I've never been very good at math," I interrupt. "Too bad I didn't get the mathematics gene."

"I'll teach you," he says. "Give me time. Everybody is good at something. Math wasn't much, but it was something. So it got me through high school and, at college, I sailed through accounting and one thing led to another until I found myself in law school specializing in corporate stuff, tax law. The things that most people, even lawyers, find incredibly boring."

My mom pipes up then. "I met your father when he was in law school. He was cute and I felt sorry for him at first. But then I could see he was gentler than any of the other boys I dated. He was struggling, though, with something inside him, and barely keeping his head above water."

My father moves back to the table and pours another shot of putrid wine into the jar. "That's exactly how it felt. That's the way I felt my whole life. I felt like if I gave up the fight, I'd drown. But I never had a chance to really find what most people call their identity. I never gave myself the opportunity.

"Flash forward to me and your mom getting married. Small ceremony, no fuss, both of us leaning on each other for support. But I was the weaker one. Your mom, she was tough."

"But emotionally unstable," my mom adds, throwing the onions into a deep pot with some corn oil and, I am glad to see, setting the big, bladed knife into the sink.

"We both thought getting married would solve all our problems. And for a while it did. I made it through law

school—just barely—while your mom supported, me working shifts at the chocolate factory."

I had never known my mother worked at a chocolate
factory. What a wonderful-sounding job.

"That lasted long enough for your father to get a real job
with a law firm."

"Dyson and Lamont. Business law. Dyson was like eighty
years old and shouted at me all the time. Told me I was the
worst lawyer he'd ever seen. They gave me all the crap
cases. I was like a bill collector, really. Hated every minute of
it. But then you came along and we both thought that now
we have real family and we'll be like a real happy-got-our-
shit-together family unit."

"Only we didn't have our shit together," my mom chimes
in again, wrestling with our damn can opener and a can of
spaghetti sauce.

"Let me help you with that," my dad says, taking the
opener and wrestling with it himself.

Turning to me he says, "I was as shitty a father as I was a
husband. Neither of you deserved that. But that was me. I
had never found—and pardon me for sounding like a cliché
—I'd never found out who I was."

The identity thing. I never knew how important it was to
him. Me, I am always thinking, if nothing else, I know *who* I
am.

"So, when I just up and left my job and left you two, I was
finally truly drowning. And I didn't want to drag you down."

I still want to shout at him. I don't know if he thinks we
could forgive him if we feel sorry for him, but not me. I am
beginning to see more clearly how I was destined to be

walked on by heavily-booted feet right from the start. "So you just disappeared?"

"I did. And I was more lost than ever. I drove for six days and ended up in this suburban town on the West Coast. No one knew me. No one cared one thing about me. And that seemed like a good start. A chance. A quick search got me a job working for an import-export company. They specialized in importing kitchen utensils and gadgets like you see on the Shopping Channel. Had to get a new license to practise law there, but they paid for it. The law exam was easy. The job, too, was easy and the pay was good. Just tax stuff. Boring. But I was good at it.

"I started to feel a little better about myself but feeling more and more like a failure for walking out on you two. It was like I was waiting for a miracle to change my sorry life. And then it happened. A professional couple with deep pockets decided to launch a lawsuit against our company. The wife had been using one of our specialty carrot peelers when it slipped and she slit open her wrists. At least that's what she said. She nearly bled to death before her husband could get her to a hospital and have her stitched up. The two of them hired a guy like Kelsey to file the suit— two million dollars, claiming the accident had ruined their relationship. The husband claimed loss of his conjugal rights and both said they were incapable of returning to their jobs due to mental pain and suffering."

My mom is quiet now. Like me, she is hearing the story for the first time. She stirs the spaghetti sauce in with the onions and dumps in a lot of garlic salt and pepper.

My dad is on a bit of a roll now. "So they sue the company

over the carrot peeler. Our hotshot top corporate lawyer starts the case but has a heart attack and dies, and the man who owns the whole frigging company comes to me and says I need to finish it. I knew next to nothing about this sort of thing. I was just a tax guy. But they're desperate and, strangely enough, the owner tells me that he has faith in me.

"So I do it. It gets ugly and weird. Really weird, right down to changes in their sex lives as a result of the wound. But the uglier it gets, the harder I fight. And in the end, they lose. We win. *I* won. It was the first time I won anything in my life. And I just saved the company two mil. So the big boss gives me this big bonus.

"And that changed me somehow. It really did. I know I was only doing my job. But I'd found the fighter in me. And right then I started thinking about coming back to make amends. To turn my life—and your lives—around."

I still want to shout "Bullshit!" but my father's newly-minted enthusiasm doesn't deserve any flak.

"But soon after that, I'm at this fancy bar with some people from the company, celebrating, and someone is fooling with their phone. They start showing this video clip of two boys fighting in a locker room. It's tilted my way and it takes a few seconds before it sinks in. It's you, John Francis. But I get really pissed off, I mean really freaking angry, when someone with his back to me looks at it and roars out loud laughing."

"What did you do?" my mom asks, knowing the story is not over.

"I started screaming at him like a maniac. I couldn't even

see his face with his back to me but I called him every insulting name I could think of and then some more that I made up on the spot."

"Who was it?" I ask.

"My boss."

"Oh, my God," my mother says.

"No, no," my dad says, with a big, broad smile. "I felt more alive than I've ever felt in my life."

Chapter Eighteen

I leave my parents sitting at the kitchen table, smiling at each other, an event I had never ever expected to see again in my lifetime. But no, my father's return does not suddenly make everything okay. Maybe it never will. But I won't reject it as a good turn of events. Lord knows, I need some good news in my life. As does my bat-happy sometimes bat-crazy mother. So be it.

After the spaghetti was consumed and the remainder of the stale wine was poured down the sink, I retreat to my room, thinking I should do my homework. But then it occurs to me I don't have any homework and I will not be going to school in the morning. It reminds me of the days of COVID-19 when school was cancelled suddenly and we all had this amazing amount of free time on our hands but then, after a short time, some of us were wishing we were back in the cozy, familiar classrooms of our youth.

This, however, is different. I am the only one who will not be going back to Memorial. Everyone else will. One door closing. Where is the other one opening?

I sit down at my IKEA desk in my room and open my laptop. Someone had forwarded me a posting of a still shot of me planking Larkin up against his locker with the caption. "Got What He Deserved!"

Oh boy, it just won't go away.

I watch some YouTube videos of teenagers doing famously dangerous and silly things involving skateboards, unicycles, mountain bikes and roller blades, and think again about all the wonderfully silly and stupid things I *didn't* do while growing up, sometimes because of my weight. To offset that, however, I revert to one of my cherished pastimes of researching famous oversized people in history. This leads me to the familiar bathtub story about Howard Taft, considered by most authorities to be the heaviest American president.

On one particular forum page contributors offer up comments like "Nero was a chubber," "John Adams was known as His Rotundity," and more. There are some notes about William the Conqueror and, of course, Henry the VIII, reminders that Elvis was certainly busting buttons before he OD'd and that Winston Churchill had a pretty good paunch going. Queen Victoria was portly in her later years and, in Hollywood, there were Orson Welles and Marlon Brando.

I use this research to remind myself I am in reasonably good company, but then start wondering if Larkin has seen the "Got What He Deserved" posting.

It's about then that my window opens. Without asking permission (naturally), Robin is lifting the sash all the way up and climbing in. It is one of those kind of nights.

I am once again thankful that my bedroom is on the first floor and my mom's is above me, on the second. Of course, it means that I am always closer to the kitchen and that Robin can visit freely when she needs some escape from her own house—which is a fairly regular thing.

"I'll bring my cutters next time and trim that azalea bush," she says by way of salutation. "It's a bit out of control."

"Hi to you, too."

"What is that monstrosity in the street, parked by your driveway?"

"I didn't notice. What do you mean?"

"Some big, hulking SUV with tinted windows. You got the FBI after you now?"

"I don't think so. Must be my father's." I hadn't really checked out his vehicle.

"Your father?"

"He's back."

"And?"

"I don't know. He's changed."

"People don't change."

This is a familiar conversation Robin and I would have when discussing most anyone from school or anyone in the news, or anyone on the planet, for that matter.

"Well, he's back and he has a story and my mom is happy and I'm kind of glad he's here even though I don't know if I can forgive him for abandoning us for all those years."

"You shouldn't. Forgiveness is a weakness. Right now, you need to be strong."

"Right now, I need all the allies I can get, blood-related or not."

Robin acquiesces. I guess that meant she concedes on that point, which is very rare.

I notice about then that she has on her sleep-over

clothes. I don't mean pyjamas or anything like that. Military cargo pants and her famous, faded Pixies sweatshirt hoodie. When things become unsettling at home for her, she retreats to my bedroom.

She is welcome to use the front door. My mom has no problems with Robin sleeping over in my room, but Robin prefers fighting it out with the azalea bush and coming in through the window. I just wasn't expecting her tonight.

Don't be too shocked to learn that she sleeps on the bed with me. Not *in* it. *On* it. I tuck myself down in the sheets like normal and she carves out a sliver of space on the side near the window, sleeping on top of the covers in her military/Pixie sleeping attire with my old *Toy Story* blanket over her.

She says we are like South America—meaning I am Argentina and she is Chile. If you've never looked at a map of the lower half of that continent, this wouldn't mean anything, but give it a look and you'll see.

"Trouble at home?" I ask.

"Yeah. I couldn't take it. Mom and Vince discussing their incompatibility. It's their favourite topic of conversation."

"I thought you liked Vince."

"Vince is okay, all things considered. As number four husband, he outshines numbers one through three, but my mom catalogues his flaws when he's not around and I'm starting to see what she sees."

"And that's not good."

"Well, it's not what you'd call domestic bliss."

Robin's mother is a classically-beautiful woman. Not someone who would ever be called cute. Beautiful in the sense that she looks like a chic woman in a fashion magazine who would be flaunting expensive jewellery. A true beauty who is also quite smart but has dumbed it down all her life, according to her daughter, to suit the men she was with. All of those men tend to be ambitious, business-type arses looking for arm candy.

Robin's mom fell for them sequentially until they arrived at a mutual understanding of their incompatibility. Not her own "biological father" (as she called him) nor the succeeding stepfathers ever took the time or energy to understand Robin and her unconventional thoughts and ways. So she's had a rough ride of it.

"Anyway," I say, "I could use the company. You're always welcome here."

"I know that. Thanks. When they get going, the two of them, I start thinking about all those pills in my mom's medicine cabinet, so I figure I better get out of Dodge."

"I'm glad you're here."

I close up my laptop, turn on the small lamp on my desk and hand Robin my *Toy Story* blanket. She takes up her position on the West Coast of South America and I tuck in on the Atlantic side.

That's when we both hear the noise coming from above.

"Jesus." Robin is the first to speak. "Your father just got home after abandoning you both and now the two of them are going at it?"

We listen to the creaking bed, the moaning, the muffled words that we're better off not hearing clearly.

"Apparently," I say. It'd been a long time since I'd heard the noises coming from above.

"You know," Robin begins, "sex is responsible for a lot of the bad shit that happens in the world."

Robin has a litany of four things that she thinks responsible for most of the ills of the world. "Sex, religion, power and money, right?" I say. These are her words—her reasons for earthly problems.

She pokes me through the blanket. "Are you making fun of me?"

I think I better keep the conversation going, if nothing else to mask the escalation of the family reunion taking place upstairs. "Well, if you take away money, everything would be free, I can understand that. And if you take away power, then nobody would try to take advantage of anyone else. And I could see doing away with religion, but we all need something to believe in. Even if it is the Pixies. But if you take away sex, the human race would end."

"And you're suggesting that's a bad thing?" Robin is dead serious, not even trying to be funny.

"Cows would all die. They can't survive without humans. Corn would revert to its most ancient weedy ancestors. There would be no more sitcoms. No poetry. No music."

"Small price to pay, I say. Now shut up and go to sleep."

The ruckus from above has come to its inevitable conclusion and it is quiet. Robin touches me on the shoulder and whispers, "Shh."

I lie there quietly, listening to her breathing slow itself into a steady rhythmic pattern, and stay awake until I am sure she is asleep.

I've always been lucky that I can fall asleep just about anywhere at any time. Just throw the mental switch and—

bang—I am off to la-la land. Tonight is no different.

Not long after the stage where I had left behind my skinny little boy self, I started reading an old psychology textbook that I had picked up at the curb from someone's trash. In it was a series of images and explanations about body type and personality. I discovered something called Sheldon's Personality Theory and realized I was supposedly evolving from something called an Ectomorph to an Endomorph. Kind of like a tadpole growing and becoming a frog.

I couldn't believe that body type could dictate personality and I'm sure that it's no longer politically correct to look at people this way. But it seemed to make sense as I grew older.

What I read was this: "Endomorphs have a round shaped body. They are sociable, relaxed, tolerant and generally happy and content. They are even-tempered, fun-loving and good humoured. They love food and affection." And, of course, chubs like *moi* could fall asleep easily even though they should be worried about certain criminal charges or grossed out from their parents screwing like rabbits just above their head.

As I begin to doze off now, though, I kind of think that Henry VIII and William the Conqueror probably don't fit neatly into Sheldon's Theory of Personality.

But I do.

Chapter Nineteen

Robin climbs out the window first thing in the morning to pee behind the azalea rather than walk upstairs to the bathroom, so then I have to persuade her to come back in and let me introduce her to my prodigal father.

"Only if you go with me to the Recovery Room. I need a pep talk from the Rev."

"What about school?"

"Forget school. I'll go later. I need to stay on track."

I know that Robin does need to stay on track, meaning avoid being tempted by whatever drug surfaces in her imagination and brings on those irrepressible cravings. "Sure, I'll go there with you. I don't have anything better to do. But first we need breakfast."

"I only eat fruit for breakfast."

"I'm sure we can find something," I say, well knowing my mother never keeps fresh fruit in the house.

"Breakfast of champions," my father says, greeting us as we walk into the kitchen. He's frying bacon on the stove. The aroma makes me dizzy. "I went out to the store first thing."

He notices Robin standing there but doesn't acknowledge her presence in the slightest. Maybe he thinks she is a figment of his imagination.

"Dad," I say (even though the word caught like dust in my throat), "this is Robin. She slept over."

He blinks like I had just spoken in a foreign language he did not understand, but then recovers enough to say, "That's really nice."

I go looking for the year-old granola box I remember we once had in the cupboard, but I guess my mom had thrown it away.

"Your mother will be down in a minute. I've got coffee if you guys want some."

I look at Robin. Coffee is a political thing for her.

As if on cue, my father says, "Organic, dark roast, fair trade," making me realize I truly don't know this man. He just uttered the only five words that could possibly have persuaded Robin to stay for breakfast.

He grabs a couple of chipped mugs from a shelf and pours us both a coffee. "The bacon is done. And I have a cheese omelette big enough for all four of us." I was sure the bacon would have scared away Robin, but she is hovering over her steaming cup of fair trade and maybe it just didn't sink in. What I had heard were the words *cheese* and *omelette*, and that's enough to send me into endomorphic bliss, so it's shaping up to be a fine non-school morning. Maybe this is the door opening.

My mom arrives in the kitchen humming something—a song from the nineties that I can't quite pin down. She looks at Robin, smiles and nods. Robin had shown up at breakfast after a sleepover any number of times and my mom, God bless her, had never said a word or asked an embarrassing question.

Dear old dad is shovelling sizzling bacon onto a serving platter and then divvying up the largest cheese omelette I'd ever seen, Not only did he go out first thing to buy grub, but he must have bought cookware as well.

Before anyone can say *alakazam* or *zippity doo dah*, we are all seated at the oblong kitchen table with the platter of cheesy eggs and bacon in the centre of the table. This endomorph chows down without a further invitation and is promptly freaked to his ankles to see Robin pick up a piece of crispy dark bacon and lift it to her mouth.

When she allows her taste buds to kick in, she utters two words—"God damn"—in a way that persuades me that she likes it very much. She eats everything on her plate before I do, and no one ever does that.

I have a number of theories about my father. One is that he has been taken over by aliens—good aliens, kindly ones who have come to earth to attempt to repair damaged lives and right a few wrongs. Or that he's had a brain transplant and is the recipient of the brain of a cheerful, generous man. He had made no references to religion so it isn't like Saul on the road to Damascus or anything like that.

But it has to be something. Maybe it's as simple as his story. One day he wins a court case and the next thing you know he's screaming nasty insults at his employer, losing his job and feeling happier than he's ever been. Who's to question this?

"Anybody want a ride in the Escalade?" he asks after I'd all but licked the bacon grease off my plate. I didn't know what an Escalade was but I am soon in the belly of the beast and happily so.

It turns out that an Escalade is a big, honking Cadillac SUV, like rich politicians ride in, and my father is chirping, "Maybe we could all drive on down to the lake. It's a beautiful morning."

I had forgotten that there even was a "lake" anywhere within driving distance. He must mean Wood Park, and Green Haven Lake. I remember going there once and only once as a kid—the skinny kid who skipped flat stones into the water until his arm ached.

"I'm going to stay right here and tidy up," my mom says. I'd never before in my life heard her use the term "tidy up."

I look at Robin. She whispers to me, "I really need to go to the Recovery Room. It'll help me get through this."

She is serious, of course.

"Robin could use a ride," I say. "I'll come, too."

"Great," my dad says. "Anywhere you like. I'll be the chauffeur."

The Escalade is this giant, tank-like vehicle with tinted windows. More Mafia than FBI or POTUS. It smells of money and my dad insists that Robin and I sit in the back seat.

It is like a small waiting room back there. There is a television and what looks like a bar built into the back of the front seat. I open a little sliding door and see only sodas and juice.

Robin grabs a bottle of orange juice and slugs it back.

"Comfortable back there?" the chauffeur asks.

"This is great," I say. "Can we go camping in this sometime?"

"Camping, sure. We can buy a tent."

"No, I mean, just drive out of town somewhere and sleep in here?"

"Sure. Whatever you want."

Robin just rolls her eyes, but then she gives him directions to the Unitarian church and we are there in no time.

She makes a point of explaining why she needs to be there and my dad just says, "I understand perfectly. Can I come in with you?"

She shrugs. "Sure. Why not?"

Reverend Kevin greets us and offers coffee which doesn't quite make the grade after that breakfast. Robin asks for her pep talk and they walk into the kitchen while my father and I sit on a couple of metal folding chairs.

I explain what the nature of the place is and a bit about Robin. He keeps saying, "I get it," and "I understand," and he seems to really mean it.

The tattoo guy and Judge Shaky are off in a corner, talking about something that seems important, so they nod at us but keep to themselves.

Robin is gone maybe five minutes when Tommy from the neighbouring jail cell shows up. "Hey, man," he says.

"Hey," I respond. "You took my advice."

"Free coffee," he says, wavering a bit but aiming for the coffee urn. "Place to hang for a few hours. Good company. Who's the suit?"

"My father," I say. He isn't wearing a suit, but he does look out of place and a bit too well-dressed.

"Nice to see a kid hanging out with his old man. Fucking family photo time."

"Something like that," I say. "Keeping out of trouble?"

"Just barely," he says, "but it's a start." And he walks over to the far end of the basement hall and turns on the wall-mounted TV to watch the morning news.

Robin returns with the Reverend in tow. She has had her pep talk and looks less like a spooked deer now.

I introduce my father, who then asks a few questions about the Recovery Room. The Reverend Kevin explains in his soft-spoken voice about the work they do. "Mostly, we're just here," he concludes. "We stay open as often as we can. We offer support. We don't try to save the world, just offer some advice, some encouragement, some place to hang out and avoid temptation."

"Does it work?" my old man asks.

"Sometimes."

"How do you fund it?"

Rev throws up his hands. "The church helps," he says, pointing upward to either the sanctuary above or to God. "Sometimes we get donations."

My dad nods. "I get it," he says again and opens his wallet. He only has a five-dollar bill.

Rev Kev is looking at the five. "We take PayPal or credit."

"American Express?"

"You betcha."

Chapter Twenty

I don't know how much my re-invented father donated to the Recovery Room but it appears to make the reverend's day. I am back to thinking more seriously about the kindly alien takeover theory.

Robin says she is going to hang here and maybe go back to school after lunch—not that she hardly ever eats lunch. I think she should go straight to school to stay out of trouble. But when Robin makes up her mind, you don't try to change it.

My dad seems quite pleased with himself as he tucks his credit card back into a spiffy-looking wallet. Despite the lightning, thunder and storm clouds in my current life, I am feeling pretty good about things. Go figure.

We don't quite make it back out the door before Judge Shaky gives my father a stare-down. They are like two old dogs sniffing the air, but then my dad suddenly breaks into a grin. He's finally, after all these years, gotten the hang of smiling.

"Judge?"

"Yep. Do I know you?"

"I was in your law school class. What was it? Torts?"

Shaky laughs. "Torts, tarts, I can't remember. That was a

long time ago. Night class, right?"

"Yes. I believe so."

"Looks like you just made the Rev rather happy."

"Who says money can't buy happiness?" my dad says, confirming the fact that the kindly aliens indeed make visitations to earth.

The Judge sets down his paper coffee cup, shakes my father's hand and then nods my way. "I hear your boy got himself in a bit of a scrape."

"Boys will be boys."

"Not when the law gets involved. I should know."

My dad now looks less sure of himself and scratches his cheek. "We are in a bit of a corner."

"Kelsey, right? It was Henry Kelsey's son that took the locker in the nose?"

"Something like that."

"Kelsey is not a man to trifle with. In fact, he's a real bastard," the judge says. "I'd had him in my courtroom back in the day. He was a young Turk, mean as a rooster that hadn't been laid."

"John Francis has been charged with assault."

"And kicked out of school," I add.

"Double double," the judge says. "What are you gonna do?"

"Court date is in a week. Guess I need to do my homework."

"Homework won't cut it against Kelsey. He's a hateful one. Born with a sharpened stick up his ass. Takes it out and pokes it in the eye of anyone gets in his way."

"I have faith in the legal system that we can get the whole

truth on the table. Extenuating circumstances."

"Your faith is unfounded. I should know. Who's the judge?"

My father looks at me. I don't have a clue.

"Probably Marianne Campbell," Shaky says. "She'd be the one to handle this. She's fair, but Kelsey will come in with more firepower than the Japanese at Pearl Harbor. Any way to keep it completely out of the court?"

"I'm gonna meet with Henry Kelsey today," my father says. He hadn't told me. "Maybe we can hash it out *mano a mano*."

"More like *mano a* wolf," Shaky says. "Watch your back."

He purses his lips, gives me a most serious look, and then turns back to my father. "Kelsey doesn't like to lose. I'd be careful."

"I will," my father says. "And I've learned a trick or two."

Back in the car, my dad opens the tinted glass of the sunroof and looks up into the blue sky. "We got a lot of catching up to do," he says. "You like to fish?"

"Never fished."

"Hike?"

"I walk to school sometimes."

I think my dad realizes whatever classic father-son list he can come up with, he is going to strike out. "What do you like to do?"

"Read," I say. "And eat. Sometimes both at the same time."

"We can do that," he says. "Read and eat. Sounds like the perfect combination. We'll come up with a plan."

"Sounds good to me."

"But first, I have to go meet with this Kelsey character."

"Don't mention that mom smashed in his windshield." I'm joking.

"She did that? Really? Your mother still has that temper?"

"She does."

"That's because she's passionate," he says, still staring up at the sky through the sunroof.

I kind of wish he hadn't said that. It makes me think of the bed creaking above my ceiling last night. No one really wants to think about their own parents having sex.

"Dad," I say. The word comes out easier this time. "You really do need to be careful with Larkin's father. If he is any-thing like his son, he likes to fool people. Make them think he's your friend, then find your weakness and go for the jugular. Larkin likes to hurt people. And he likes to let you know he's out there waiting for a chance to pounce. He waited for Brady to taunt him and then waited until he was in a small group with only his cronies around to watch."

"But you were there. He miscalculated."

"He assumed I would be a marshmallow. Stand there and let it happen."

"But you didn't."

"Somebody had to do something."

"And that's where you came into the picture."

"Larkin had this thing he did around school. For the kids that were scared of him, it drove them crazy. It psyched out some of the teachers too. He'd wait until everyone was in class and he'd hang back in the hallway and then walk down the hall, dragging a pen against all the metal lockers – this loud click, click, click that let everyone know it was him, just taking his sweet time and trying to unnerve anyone weak enough to be his potential victim. It was a small thing but effective. He'd show up to whatever class he was late for and then put on that smarmy fake smile of his, apologize profusely and the teachers wouldn't say a thing."

"We had a couple of his types when I was in school."

"Every school has them. But I think Larkin is a one of a kind. What if he got it from his father?"

"I guess I'll find out. I'm going to head over there right after I drop you off."

"I want to go with you."

"No way. I'm not going to let him browbeat you. God knows what the man would say."

"I can take it. Sticks and stones, remember?"

"Absolutely not."

But I won't get out of the car when we are parked in our driveway. "I'm doing this," I say. I am being my mother's son, I guess. I have made up my mind I'm not going to let my father go into the wolf's den alone.

"Please, just go inside."

I don't budge. One thing about being a personage of some considerable weight, you can generally rest assured that no one else is going to physically try to make you move.

"Son of a gun," my father says, closing the sunroof. It suddenly feels pretty good looking out at the world from behind the smoky, tinted glass.

Chapter Twenty-One

But then my dad shuts off the engine and goes into the house without saying anything so I think maybe he is calling off the whole expedition. I decide it could be a trick, so I hold my ground, sitting there on the comfortable black leather seat with the smell of an expensive new car filling my nostrils.

About fifteen minutes later, though, he emerges from the house in a suit, with my mother in tow. They kiss on the doorstep like a pair of newlyweds and my mom straightens his tie. It's a golden moment as far as I am concerned.

As my father approaches the car, I can see why he had changed. His clothes reek of power. Cuff links, a silk tie and a tie pin. All very tastefully understated, of course. Man of the world. But the expensive tailored suit paired with the expensive black car now forms quite a cocktail of old-style masculine businessman prowess.

As we back out of the driveway, I want to roll down the tinted window and hope that I would be seen with this man of the world who is my father, but the streets are mostly empty.

When we pull into the lot at the business park, there is no sign of the damaged Range Rover. I guess it would look bad to leave it sitting there with the battered door, smashed windows and those little cube chunks of safety glass sprayed around on the pavement.

Dad seems plenty confident still and has not said a word to me about staying in the car when he goes in. "Showtime," he says, putting the car in park and checking his tie in the mirror.

As I get out of the car, I tuck in my shirt as best I can and rather wish I had taken the time to make myself look a little more presentable.

Inside, a receptionist who looks like a movie actress smiles and says, "What can I do for you two gentlemen?" which is a first. No one had ever in my entire life grouped me into that category. Dad's suit must be enough flash for the two of us.

"I'd like to speak with Henry Kelsey," he says, cool as the coolest cucumber in the field.

"Do you have an appointment?"

"I'm afraid I don't, but this is of the utmost importance."

He hands her a business card as if this is what he does every day of his life to open doors to the inner worlds of law and commerce. She looks at the card, scrunches up her pretty brow and then sends a text message.

Several quiet seconds pass which allow my father and me to study the enormous abstract art on the walls. There is one large painting, all of black, grey and murky green, that looks like something a really disturbed person would create if given a couple of buckets of unusable old warehouse paint.

Surprisingly, the secretary interrupts the brief art review

and says, "Mr. Kelsey says you can go in now."

My dad doesn't seem the slightest bit surprised. He gives a small tug to his suit jacket and offers me a confident nod as I follow him through a large mahogany door.

Henry Kelsey is not seated at his desk, but is standing by the floor-to-ceiling glass wall looking out at the parking lot, presumably at the parking space where his Range Rover would normally have been parked.

"Mr. Cummings," he says without turning towards us.

"Mr. Kelsey."

Mano a mano so far. No one is acknowledging my presence. Fine by me. I will be the fly on the wall.

There is an awkward silence. At least, it feels awkward to me. Neither man speaks and it seems like some kind of test I don't fully understand, but it gives me time to study the man who is Larkin's father.

Another expensive suit. But not above the league of my father's, I reckon. Several rings on the fingers of both hands that seem a bit much. As he adjusts the cuff of his shirt sleeve, an oversized silver watch without any numbers catches a beam of sunlight and flashes it around the walls and ceilings. Very impressive.

Kelsey is a big man. Tall, barrel-chested, larger than life, supporting a jowly face and professional hair. There are diplomas on the walls, and photos of himself and other men in suits—obviously important men—shaking hands with Kelsey.

"And this, I presume, is your son," he says at length.

"John Francis," my dad says. "We came to try to sort out this misunderstanding."

I like the fact that he said "we."

"John Francis," Kelsey echoes, not really turning my way but offering a cynical smile to a point on the wall above my head. "The boy who injured my son."

"Well, he was attempting to prevent your son from doing some real physical harm to another student."

"That sounds like a fabrication to me."

"I believe it to be the truth," Dad says, but I decide I should speak for myself.

"Larkin was bashing Brady Quinn's head into a concrete floor when I pulled him off."

That bastard smiles again, but now he looks me in the eye. It is a look that drained the blood right down to my toes. "You pulled him off, did you?"

"Others were in the room," my father says. "There were witnesses."

Kelsey walks across the room and sits down at his desk. A man sitting behind a big-ass desk is a power play—at least, it is in the movies. He makes a little tent out of his fingers. "We've already interviewed those in the room. They have said no such thing."

This doesn't surprise me.

He turns to my father. "We did what we call a deposition." It's meant to be a slap in the face, as if my lawyer father wouldn't know the term.

"What about the coach?"

"He gave a statement as well. There was no such thing as Larkin attacking another boy."

Coach Simms had not observed the first part of the scene. The other boys had. They lied to keep their asses clean. No one at school wants Larkin for an enemy.

"There is more to the video," I interject. "Harrison filmed the whole thing from the beginning."

"Ah, the video. You'll be pleased to know we contacted the original internet site and insisted they take it down. They were willing to oblige. It would end the embarrassment for all concerned."

Yeah, I think, after it had been seen by half the planet, copied and reposted a hundred times. Maybe a thousand times. But never in its complete version. Internally, I am beginning to squirm.

My father begins to speak. He carefully repeats what I had told him about the event but using cautious formal and even legal terms. He offers up reasons why the charges against me were not legitimate. He cites precedents, logic.

Kelsey sits silently, using his eyes to drill into him. The more my father speaks, the more I can feel the wind spilling from his sails. I can sense him losing confidence in himself and faltering.

Kelsey just sits there.

I try to see the Larkin in him. But he is not quite the same. Larkin is always easy for me to read. This is different. He is not exactly his father's son. Here is a much higher level of sophistication. There is something about this guy and his ability to stay cool, to manipulate this or probably any other situation, that scares the shit out of me.

And Henry Kelsey is more than getting to my father.

"Let's go," I say to him finally. "We've said our piece."

My dad looks my way, then back at Mr. Kelsey. Finally, he wipes a hand across his mouth and asks, "What do you intend to do?"

Kelsey flips his hands out like the wings of some predatory bird. "I've already done what is needed to be done. Convince authorities to press charges, provide evidence. Now it's just a matter of letting the legal system do its job."

"And you're suing the school?" I add.

"The school, the school board. Negligence. Someone has to take a stand on these things. Now, I'd like to thank you both for taking the time to come by today. I really do appreciate it."

My father begins to move towards the door. I look up at a photo on the wall of Henry Kelsey and realize the man he is shaking hands with is an astronaut. All my life I'd wanted to meet an astronaut—someone who'd seen our world from space. Henry Kelsey had been able to shake hands with an astronaut.

As we walk through the outer office, I stare at that ugly abstract painting and realize it reminds me of something called a Rorschach test that I'd read about in that psychology text I'd found in the trash. A blotted ink blob. Shrinks ask subjects what they see in the blob of ink. What I see just now is some kind of large black dog attacking a rabbit. Or maybe it is a mouse.

Chapter Twenty-Two

I had a dream that night. There was that big black dog, right out of the painting, chasing me. It wasn't a real dog of course. Dogs have always liked me. Even mean dogs. Robin always said I could probably tame wild animals profession-ally if I wanted to, but I had replied that I didn't think that was a viable career plan.

So, in my dream, the dog was a kind of horror/cartoony dog and he was bigger than me and had red eyes. I was run-ning through a dark forest. (Are you with me yet, Dr. Freud?) And I was losing ground as the power of my legs was diminishing.

But here's the thing. I was thin. Not waifish paper-thin like Robin but, you know, moderately slim.

But then I wake up when some terribly strange sound fills my ears. It's the sound of my father crying.

Not good.

It is an outright cry of anguish followed by sobs, and then the muffled voice of my mother soothing him.

This is not good at all. The thin veneer of bravado that he had shown at first in Kelsey's office had evaporated, I guess. Now this.

In the morning there's no bacon and eggs, no French

toast or pancakes. My parents are a subdued and despondent pair at breakfast, and I guess that the glory of the family reunion has worn off already.

I keep thinking I should eat some stale corn flakes and get ready for school. But, of course, I am not wanted there. Not even permitted there. From the look on my father's face, I am pretty sure there is no father/son fishing expedition happening today, or anytime soon either.

My mother, strangely enough, is trying to be a bit of a cheerleader, commenting on the good weather and the fact that she was now able to get a few more hours at the beauty supply store where she works part-time. My father says he is going to "go downtown" to see about getting employment at H&R Block, which is some kind of strip mall store where they do the taxes for people who walk in off the street. It sounds like a crappy job for a man who drives a Cadillac Escalade and generously donates money to places like the Recovery Room.

I take my time eating, still thinking about the thin version of me running from the black dog, but trying to keep my mind off the courtroom appearance coming up in seven days.

When my father is about to go out the door, he kisses my mother and then touches me on the shoulder in a way that is meant to be fatherly, I think, but it gets me worried that maybe he is about to disappear from our lives forever again.

His hand is on the door when I say, "Wait."

He turns and looks at me.

"Mom's working today. I'm home. I'll cook dinner. What do you want?"

He acts a little stunned. "I don't know. Anything."

"Can you be more specific? Think of something you haven't had in a long time."

He pauses and seems to be thinking about it. "Cabbage soup," he finally says. "My mother used to make it when I was little."

I'd never heard of cabbage soup. It sounds awful, like something starving Russian peasants would have to eat if there was nothing left. "I'll look up the recipe on the internet and get right on it."

He smiles a soft, defeated smile then and tosses three twenties on the table. "For the ingredients. You'll have to go shopping."

The only soup I'd ever prepared was Campbell's chunky beef out of a red can. Guess it was time I learned how to make soup from scratch. Maybe it would come in handy in prison or wherever I was likely headed. They'd probably let me be a cook if I was good.

I could see myself ladling out some kind of gristly stew onto those metal trays I'd seen in the prison movies my mom liked so much. A fight would break out where two tough guys are vying for power and they'd throw their trays with my stew or cabbage soup at each other.

Once my father is gone, my mom sits down across from me and stirs sugar into her black coffee. "Your father's a good man," she says. "He's got his good days and his bad days, though. When I met him, he told me he was manic depressive."

It had never really occurred to me that Mom's explanation of him being "mentally unhealthy" may have had some truth to it. "You mean bipolar?"

"Same thing. He kept saying that he thought he would grow out of it. And I kept waiting. But then he left."

"How come you just accepted the fact he was back?"

"Because I still love him. Because he's good for me."

It's true. My mom is a much-improved person since he returned. The Slugger is retired to a hallway closet. She now has moments of appearing to be genuinely happy. It is almost like having a normal mother.

"If you get convicted and get sent away, I don't think he can handle it."

"What about you?"

"I don't think I can handle it, either."

I don't know what to say at that point. Part of me has already accepted that whatever is going to happen will happen no matter what I say or do. My lawyer father had shown up and given me some false glimmer of hope, but I have a whole posse of people against me now—against us.

That posse is headed by Larkin and his old man. And there is Dr. Mantel Morgan and the entire school board, who are hoping that I will be a suitable scapegoat now that I've been "terminated" from the system. No allies from the locker room, that's for sure. Even the damn coach came out against me.

Boy with a problem. That's me. Big problem for a big boy.

Strangely, I have already factored all of this in and assume that, with things stacked that high against me, I am screwed. But I hadn't factored in how this was going to drag down others. Not just my reunited mom and dad, but Robin, too. She'd see herself as a failed student advocate, failed friend, failed saviour of the underdog—that would be me. Would she slip back into drugs? You bet.

Mom goes looking through the kitchen cabinet until she finds a little wooden box. She sets it on the table in front of me.

"What is it?" I ask.

"Recipe box. Your father made it."

She riffles through it until she comes to a certain index card, which she pulls out and sets down on the table. The ink is faded and it is quite stained "Cabbage soup," she says. "I used to make it for him when we were living together in college. We were broke and it was cheap. I gotta go to work. You be okay?"

"I'll be great," I say, thinking that the wonderful thing about being an endomorph is that we have the propensity to be moderately cheerful even in the most dire situations, come hell or high water.

When my mom is gone, I make myself a grilled cheese sandwich, realizing I needed something more than stale cereal to sustain me. After all, I have shopping to do and soup to cook, and I have to make it through this lonely day on my own without thinking about all the bad shit about to happen.

But I burn the sandwich, which, despite my cheerful nature, puts me in a foul mood.

Chapter Twenty-Three

You never think much about what it's like to be really alone until, well, you are really alone. My mom is off to her crappy paying job at the beauty store. My sorry dad, tail tucked between his legs, is probably begging for that job at H&R Block. I try texting Robin but get nothing—not unusual for her. Every other kid my age is at school, trying to get through another day.

Me, I am alone in my kitchen doing a totally unconvincing job of pretending to be Jamie Oliver. Why does school, now a veritable unattainable dream, seem so appealing? Don't answer that. I know. It is the thing I can't have.

I decide cooking can wait. I walk out the front door and across the lawn to seek counsel from the neighbourhood guru. After hefting myself up those steep wooden steps, I reach for the doorbell and hear the familiar sound of chimes coming from inside.

Jake Jackson looks a little droopy-eyed when he emerges from his cave. "I hope I'm not disturbing you, Mr. Jackson."

"I was just working on my chakras," he says, smiling. "It can wait. I can see from the look on your face you have some things on your mind. Sit."

Sitting on Jake Jackson's porch on a crisp windless morning like this is probably as good as it can get for a rudderless fool like me at this nexus in his life.

"Spill," he says. Mr. Jackson always picks unusual verbs. This confuses many people in the community, but not me.

I spill. Tell him the story so far.

"So I can see you have one of those plus and minus lists going," he says. "You have a father back and that's a big number for your plus list. Maybe you shouldn't focus so much on the minuses."

"I see your point. But it's hard not to. I think I'm dragging plus-side father into his own negative territory."

"Understood. If we could only control our thoughts, discipline our silly brain to set aside negativity and get on with it."

I suppose that most kids or most anyone on the street listening to Jake Jackson under my circumstances would think he is a flake or a bullshit artist, but his words often make good sense to me. He is the one who told me to study all the images on the internet of Chinese Buddhas from every century I could find. And I did. Most all were on the plump side, most were smiling. This cheered me immensely until I dug a little deeper and discovered that the real Buddha—Gautama Buddha from India—was probably as skinny as a toothpick with skin, often starving himself to avoid the pleasures of the world before achieving enlightenment.

"But those images of the happy, beefy Buddha made you feel better about yourself, right?" Jake Jackson had said.

"Yes," I had agreed.

"Then it did you some good. Happiness is always transitory and life is short, so you have to grab onto all you can before you move on to the next plane of existence."

It could have been a beer commercial for Buddhists.

This morning, however, Jake seems a little more introspective than usual. It could be the interrupted chakra work. I sit for a minute and let the silence linger. I know for a fact that Jake is a big fan of silence.

Silence is not working as a salve for my anxiety this morning, though.

"Do you hear that?" Mr. Jackson asks, just as I am about to get up and leave.

I listen. Then I hear it. It is a bird singing. I look around at the trees but can't see it.

"Yes. The bird. It's singing."

"Good ear. A tiny little chickadee, singing his heart out."

In biology we learned that male birds sang mostly to stake out territory or to warn of predators. But I have a feeling that this is not the morning lesson I am looking for from my wise, pontificating neighbour.

"Tiny bird, big voice," I say.

"You have that right. He sings because he is meant to sing. Do you do much singing?"

"Only in the shower. I can't sing very well. I was even asked to leave glee club."

"They still have glee club?"

"They did until the funding cutbacks."

"Still, a shower singer sings not because of the water but because something wells up inside him. Do you remember what was welling up inside you when you sang?"

"It was just the words to a song I heard on the radio."

"Singing soothes the soul. The chickadee knows that."

Not according to science, I want to say, but I never diss Mr. Jackson when he is on a roll, and, besides, his malarkey almost always makes me feel better.

"Do you remember what I told you before?"

He'd told me any number of things both directly and metaphorically. It is hard to pick. "Water runs downhill?"

He nods. "Yes, it does. But I was thinking of Sun Tzu. And Sun Tzu had more to say."

I can't remember who Sun Tzu was—one of the ancient Chinese sages, of course—but I can't keep them straight.

I always find it funny that, in Mr. Jackson's world, wisdom always comes from Asia. Never North America or Europe. Usually one needs to look to India, China, Japan or Nepal for wisdom. Maybe that explains why things are so messed up where I live.

Jackson, himself, however, grew up in Wales, in a city called Swansea. His father was a traditional folksinger who married a rich girl from New Jersey, and they moved to Sri Lanka before the father had a vision that his calling was in the world of VHS video rental chain stores. That had brought them to live in a nearby town where wealth had come easily for the Jackson family.

Young Jacob was raised in relative luxury with homeschooling under the tutelage of his hippie mother and folksinger-turned-entrepreneur father. I'd heard the story several times, but the "lesson" attached is often different with each telling.

"Good luck is always karma from a previous life," my mentor now pontificates. "Things happen because of some grand plan that mere mortals cannot possibly comprehend."

He pauses and closes his eyes, waiting for the little chickadee to sound off again, as if that is a cue to continue. "Destiny and free will create the perfect cocktail."

I find that last utterance a little confusing, but then Mr. Jackson is a fan of fusing opposites to suit his eclectic view of the universe.

He and I are both now drifting in thought, as we do when we sat like this, with long interludes of silence interspersed with birdsong. "Remind me again of what Sun Tzu said about hard times," I prompt him.

"Well, for starters, Sun Tzu probably wasn't even a single person. It's just a kind of composite name for all the people who contributed to *The Art of War* manuscript."

That in itself is pretty damn confusing, but I don't want to interrupt the flow of the conversation.

"Sun Tzu said this: sometimes the world is with you and sometimes it is against you. It's nothing personal. It's just the way things are."

I well understand the way things currently *are* in my world and it isn't all that pretty. "I'd say the world is currently against me."

How the world can be against a minor player like me in the big scheme of things, or even *why* the world would care, elude me. "What have I done to turn the 'the world' against me, anyway?"

Mr. Jackson smiles that gentle, knowing smile. "According to your story, you dared to challenge the scheme of things. You upset the apple cart. To paraphrase Mr. Eliot, 'You dared to disturb the universe.'"

I look up towards the tree where the bird is singing again, marking its territory, warning of a cat in the neighbourhood, perhaps, or simply singing for the sake of singing. And then a small light bulb, not much more than forty watts, goes off in my head. "I did, didn't I? Why did I do that?"

"You exerted your free will against the inexorable forces of a power-hungry individual who deserved to be taken down."

"I wasn't thinking that at the time."

"Of course not. The karmic energy was working through you. You were chosen as the instrument."

"I kind of wish I hadn't been chosen."

I want to ask exactly *who* is doing the choosing. But I know that would take a fairly long explanation about the multitudinous definitions of God. "So what do I do now?"

"Ah. Yes. That's where Sun Tzu comes in. He says, when the world is against you—as appears to be your current circumstances—you should retreat and wait for the energy of the world to be in your favour, to assist rather than fight against you."

"Retreat?"

"Yes. Or, in this case, do nothing."

"Nothing?"

"Nothing is sometimes much better than something. You need to let the wheel turn. Don't fight it."

"Well, it was fighting that got me into this."

"Of course it was. Now, you should hang back and see."

Robin would have argued with this. She is a fighter. Everything is a fight. She wants to fix the world and she believes she has to fight to do it. She is angry every day at all the wrongful things in the world and wants to fight to make changes.

"But me? Now? Do nothing? Really?"

"Really," Mr. Jackson repeats. "But not *nothing* nothing. You'll need to keep yourself occupied. Just don't try to solve your problem. Your subconscious is already working on a solution and I feel it is getting in sync with the wheel, with the universal forces that lined up against you but will soon perhaps be in your favour."

"Does there always have to be a perhaps?"

"There is always a perhaps. But now I have to get back to my chakras. I'm so pleased, though, we were able to have this little session."

"But what should I do in the meantime?"

"Simple tasks."

"I was going to make cabbage soup," I say. "Would that work?"

"Cabbage soup," Mr. Jackson repeats, his face cracking into a broad smile like I'd just come up with something as brilliant as $E = mc^2$. "Cabbage soup is the perfect antidote to your situation."

Chapter Twenty-Four

I bid Mr. Jackson goodbye and head off towards the super-market with my dad's $60 in my pants pocket, thinking that this is the first time in my life I have ever had that much money in my possession. The weather is good and I now hear more birds singing. In fact, it seems like an entire orchestra of them.

As Mr. J would advise, I am trying to "be in the moment." The ever-present present which is always so damn hard to hold onto.

The only intruders are my thoughts. The worry-warriors. Worries about Robin, my mother, and my dad probably begging at this very minute for that tax job.

As to me, what lies ahead, lies ahead. A road paved for me with bad intentions. *Stay focused on the soup*, I counsel myself. *Make sure you buy the necessary ingredients on the list in your pocket.*

That's when I sense something coming up behind me. I expect it is some innate sixth sense handed down to me from my Paleolithic or Neanderthal ancestors. Some beast is about to pounce. Some monstrous, hungry animal—that wild black dog of my dreams, maybe, or a sabre-toothed tiger. Or maybe a woolly mammoth is about to crush me and rip the flesh from my bones.

The hair stands straight up on my neck as I hear the low, throaty roar of a muscle car with an illegally-customized exhaust system. The black car stops inches from my elbow, with one tire squeezed up and over the curb.

It's Larkin's Mustang. Larkin at the wheel. He appears to be alone.

The passenger window rolls down. The wolf leans over. "Get in the car," he snarls.

I keep on walking. *Ignore the son of a bitch*, I counsel myself. *Think of something happy. An extra-large cheese sandwich swirls into my mind. A largish pizza with the works.* Why, I wonder, is it called "the works" anyway?

"John Francis Cummings," he says, a bit louder now, as if he believes I'm just wearing earbuds and not really hearing him. Both the front and back wheels of the Mustang are now up over the curb as he paces me, that ugly low rumble of the car now sounding more threatening than ever. And me thinking how odd that he is using my full name without any adjectives of his own thrown in.

I keep walking, silently repeating the mantra, *Extra cheese.* Those two words spool through my thoughts to keep me calm. Should I run? No, running would be futile. Maybe race up to someone's door and plead to be let in? Not my style. Running in any form, for any purpose, is not my strong suit. What if no one is home?

And even if I do run, I'd appear to be the coward I truly am. I wouldn't want that. Why, at this moment, do appearances seem so vitally important?

I sneak a look in Larkin's direction and then notice he is

looking at me and not at the curbside maple tree directly in his path. *Oh boy, this will be good*, I think. *Let nature be my ally and saviour.*

At the last split second, Larkin sees the tree. Stops the car as I keep walking, diverting myself around the maple. He suddenly gets out, stands there in the street looking as mean and angry as a teenage savage can. "Get in the fucking car!" he shouts.

I take a deep breath and turn to look at him. He repeats the command. Only it's evolved into a question. This time it's, "Will you please get into the fucking car?"

I don't exactly know why, but I stop walking, back shuffle a few feet from the protection of father maple and get into the fucking car.

Larkin settles himself back into the driver's seat and looks at me with what I take to be anger and frustration, served up with muscles tightening in his thick neck and bulging arms. He jams the transmission into reverse. We drop back onto the pavement. He slams the gearshift into first and squeals the tires like they do in the chase scenes in movies.

We are racing down my street now and he's pounding his fist on the steering wheel. "Damn it to hell," he says to the windshield as I wonder exactly why I chose to ignore my ancestral memory dictating flight over fight. I have no intention of fighting. My fighting days are over.

But apparently, so are my flight days. As noted, I was never a runner, especially not someone who runs out of fear.

"Where are we going?" I ask.

"Shut up and let me drive."

He drives. I stay shut up. The tension is high. My driver is sucking back snot and clenching his teeth. There is much that is appropriately primitive and hostile about him, but I figure, I'm here now. The game is in play. *Cheese*, I tell myself. *Extra cheese. In the kingdom of cheese, there are no heroes.* Not a one. What will be will be.

We end up at the river by the abandoned brick building where a once-profitable electronics company made hand-held solar calculators and cheap digital watches until the jobs all went to China. *How convenient*, I think, *how clichéd*. Back parking lot behind an abandoned factory, with the added attraction of a dirty river to deposit a body, perhaps.

Larkin drives around the old parking lot, dodging abandoned, rusty shopping carts and mouldy stuffed furniture dropped here by environmentally-unconscious citizens, until he finds appropriate parking between two hulking, rusted and overflowing dumpsters.

He pulls in, kills the ignition and sits breathing hard while staring malevolently at his thumbs on the steering wheel.

"This shit has got to stop," he says finally.

"What shit is that?" I ask, all smart-alecky.

"The shit you got us into."

Us? He used the word us. "I'm not sure I know what you mean."

"Don't be so ignorant."

"All I did was keep you from giving Brady brain damage. And I thought it was you being ignorant, not me."

The words just spill out. There isn't a lot of pre-thought

going into it, but I figure that if I am headed to a watery grave, I have a right to stand up for myself in some manner suited to a 1960s movie about teenage ruffians.

"Brady deserved it."

"He usually does," I concede.

"But this has gotten entirely out of hand."

"I couldn't agree more." Now we suddenly, most strangely, seemed to be in sync.

"My father," he suddenly blurts. "My father has got this whole thing really really fucked up."

I let the words steep for a few seconds. Larkin is angry at his father.

"He insists we make sure you get convicted and get a stiff penalty. And on top of that, he's suing the school board. It's only going to draw more attention to the whole mess."

Larkin is clearly worried about himself. But my involvement means that I am still the source of the problem.

"It has rather escalated," I agree.

"That damn video. Everyone has seen it. You with your sweaty carcass jammed up against me. You beating up on me, for god's sake. Do you know what that looks like?"

I know exactly what it looks like. "Sorry I didn't have time to politely negotiate before you cracked Brady's skull."

"You have no idea what that made me look like."

Well, I do have an idea. It made big Larkin look like a freaking high school jock who couldn't hold his own against the class pudge in an after-gym-class tussle. "I don't know what came over me," I add, half in jest.

"This isn't funny. Everyone has seen it. It's still out there. It's going viral in Russia, god dammit."

"I didn't know," I say, even though I had guessed as much. I'd seen it being reposted in the Czech Republic and Poland, so why not Russia?

"It was Harrison's idea. Posting the video. I didn't really know about it until it was too late. It makes me look weak. It makes me look..." but he doesn't finish the sentence.

People have nasty minds and say any old shit on the internet. I am suddenly beginning to see how this could get to a guy like Larkin.

"My father can't give it up. When he saw it, he went through the roof. You don't know my father. He thinks he can fix anything. Control everything. Or punish anyone. He thinks he can use money or the law to get his way."

"What does he want?"

"Revenge."

"On me?"

"On you. Your family. The school. It's what he does. He wants to prove a point. He wants to win."

I hadn't really thought all that much about the father-son thing. I had met Mr. Kelsey. And he is as big a turd as has ever floated down that dirty river in front of us. But I had assumed, like father like son. Now I am seeing something a little bit different.

"So, you're telling me you didn't bring me down here to beat the crap out of me?"

He chuffed—a half laugh, half snort. "I'd still like to. But it wouldn't change a damn thing. Ever since that day, it seems like nothing's working out for me."

"I thought you were the golden boy. Everything always worked out for you."

"No. Not anymore. This whole thing has turned my life to shit and it just keeps getting shittier."

I think he actually wants me to feel sorry for him.

"My girlfriend broke up with me."

"Which one?"

"Lisa."

"Why?"

"She was embarrassed to be seen with me."

"That sucks. What else?"

"Everything. Kids laugh when I come down the hall. People stare at me on the street."

"They'll get over it. You'll get over it."

"I don't know, man. I can't take it anymore."

"Tell your father to give up on the school board. Tell him to drop the charges on me."

It is now the obvious thing to do. It had never really occurred to me how badly this had turned out for Larkin. I want to say something silly like *what goes around comes around,* or give him a little Jacksonish sermon on karma, but the river still looks dirty, cold and dark, and I think there is a chance I'll end up there yet.

There is no doubt about it. Larkin is a hurting unit. Vulnerable in a way that I could never have imagined. I want to tell him he got what he deserved. Instead, I say, "Your father must be a piece of work."

"He's been on my case since I was little. I always had to be the top. The best. If I didn't come up to his standards, he'd..." Larkin trails off again.

"Beat you?"

He shakes his head. "He doesn't have to. Never did. He

drove my mom away. Didn't need to beat her either. Words are his weapons. I've been scared of him most of my life and I don't think he ever once laid a hand on me."

"So you decided to take it out on the rest of the world."

"Fuck you. Don't go getting all preachy here. I'm looking for your help."

"Jesus. You are looking for *my* help?"

"Yes, dammit."

"What do you want me to do?"

He handed me a cell phone. "Take this."

It's a cheap cell phone. The type they call a burner. Larkin thumbs it and the famous video pops up. There I am pushing him into a locker, belly to back, arms locked around him as I slam the back of his head with the front of my skull.

"So what?" I say. "I've seen this."

"Yeah, that's what everyone saw. And I do mean everyone. But now look at this."

He taps the screen again with his knuckle. And there it is. The whole thing. Larkin slamming Brady, taking him down and bouncing his head off the floor.

"Harrison told me he didn't have it anymore," he says.

"He doesn't. But I do. He sent it to me that night. I told him to erase all but the end. In case I needed it to get out of hot water. I also told him *not* to post anything. But the bastard did anyway."

"And you want what out of me?"

"Do it. Put the whole thing online."

"You'll end up like me," I say. "Morgan will kick you out of school just like me. Zero tolerance, remember? 'Terminated', he calls it now. Final. Nice and neat."

"Fuck it. Let him terminate me."

We sit in silence for at least a full minute. I half-expect that this is some kind of trap, a joke, a crazy maniacal scene where Larkin will turn on me at any minute.

But the look on Larkin's face tells me otherwise. No, he isn't going to cry. That would have turned the universe inside out. His proposal is outrageous, though. And he is asking *me* to get *him* out of a jam. That is unthinkable. Maybe the whole thing *is* a trap of some sort. I know better than to trust Larkin.

But, like I always say, I can handle the bullies. Larkin is a card-carrying, dyed-in-the wool version.

Maybe his father has that same skill, coupled with being a liar and a cheat. Those are the ones who really get my goat. I'd met the man and studied his scaly hide. But he is a big man and no doubt way more conniving than I could be in twelve lifetimes. A most formidable enemy.

Larkin sucks back some more snot. Maybe he had come close to crying. "Somebody messed up his car the other day," he said. "Smashed his windshield and bashed the door. He's totally pissed off that it didn't get caught on camera. He's driving the cops wild, demanding they figure out who did it. I can't help but think about how good that must have felt to whoever did the damage."

I can't believe he just said those words. I guess that's why I blurt it out. "That was my mom."

Larkin is staring straight ahead now. He is wide eyed. "Fucking beautiful," he says. "You lucky dog."

Chapter Twenty-Five

Well, I probably shouldn't have told him about my mom and her kinship to the Louisville Slugger, but my pride in my family got the better of me. But why would I suddenly trust Larkin just because he was playing it vulnerable?

I am still holding the phone in my hand. Here it is, the evidence that doesn't exactly show me innocent but at least explains why I did what I did. "Who else has seen this?"

"No one."

"I say we show it to your father."

"No way."

"You said you wanted me to post it. That's not gonna help improve your reputation, I'm sure. Certainly won't get you Lisa back."

"I don't want Lisa back. She's shallow and she was using me."

"Using you?"

"Yeah. She wanted to be seen with me. She wanted to talk up our relationship. But there was no relationship. Don't you get it?"

No, of course, I don't get it. A guy like Larkin and a guy like me live on two completely different planets with different gravitational rules.

"Look," I say, "if we show this to your father and he drops the charges, no one will have to see it. I'll just shut up about the real story and maybe, just maybe, I can convince Mantel Morgan to let me back in school if the charges are dropped."

"That's what you care about? Getting back into school?"

"Yes," I assert. "That and an apology."

I'm joking, of course. I really don't care one bit about an apology. I just want some semblance of my life back.

"You want me to freaking apologize?" Larkin sounds like I had asked him to do something unthinkable.

"Forget it. I don't care about the apology. Let's just take this to your father."

"He'll go through the roof."

"Because you smacked Brady around?"

"No, because someone caught it on video."

"He'll see it if I post it on social media anyway." I at least have logic on my side.

"Fuck it. Okay. But I think we need someone else in the room. If it's just you and me, he'll find a way to get to me. He always does. And he'll tear into you, too."

"I've met the man, remember?"

"But you don't know the half of it. He can be a monster."

"Then we need a monster tamer," I counter. "Someone else in the room, like you say, so he can't explode without an outside observer to bear witness."

Larkin looks at me with his hands out wide now. "Who?"

"Robin Sparrow. Official student advocate."

"Skeletor?"

"Skeletor." I hold Larkin's phone up and punch in her number.

~

Robin is sitting in front of the school when we pull up to the curb. I can see her recognize Larkin's car as we approach.

I roll down the window. "Looks like I need your help again."

Larkin leans over and attempts to smile at Robin, and it looks like she is about to spit in his face.

"It's okay, really," I say. "Larkin and I have made up. We're a kind of team now and we want you on our team."

"I have bear spray," she says, leaning in past me and glaring at Larkin.

"Great," he says, surprisingly nonchalant. "You may need it."

With a bit more coaching on my part, Robin gets in the back of the car and lights a cigarette. I give her a dirty look. She glares back. "Your buddy from jail gave me a few smokes. He said it would calm my nerves."

I was the one who had told Tommy to start hanging out at the Recovery Room. Now this. He had lured Robin back into smoking, something she had given up along with the pills.

I lean back and grab the lit cigarette from her fingers, snuff it out on my palm and then throw it out the window.

Robin glares some more. "I thought you called me for help. Now you're giving me shit and fucking up the environment."

She pulls out another cigarette, and I guess Larkin sees it in the rear-view mirror because he pushes in the car's cigarette lighter. When it pops out, he holds it up for Robin.

I wave the smoke away and lower the window again, but let the girl have her nicotine. And then I explain what is going down.

"So I'm just along for the shit show?" she asks.

Larkin looks back at her from his mirror again. "You don't know what you're getting into."

"Sounds like another male pissing contest."

"Something like that," I say. "But you have to be Switzerland."

"I'd rather be Canada."

"Canada won't cut it for this battle. We need the ultimate neutrality."

"Not really my forté."

"Then just be there. Watch and listen and make sure Larkin's father senses that you've got your wits about you."

"And bear spray," she adds.

~

The receptionist recognizes Larkin, naturally, but gives a curious once-over to Robin Sparrow and me.

"Your father is in an important meeting with a client," she says before Larkin even asks anything.

Larkin turns to me. "He's always in an important meeting with a client."

The woman at the desk presses a single button on a black box. Not more than three seconds later she tells Larkin, "Ten minutes. He'll see you in ten minutes." They must have some kind of code between them.

It's a long ten minutes. We sit. Larkin fidgets with that

phone, the one that has the video. Robin takes out another cigarette and puts it to her lips, but doesn't light it. I worry that she's taken up smoking again not because of Tommy but because she's worried about me. Collateral damage. Now, maybe I am getting her deeper into it.

I pick up some kind of business magazine with articles about billionaires. Jeff Bezos. Mark Zuckerberg, Elon Musk, Michael Bloomberg and an assortment of rulers of empires that sell luxury items. They all look like unlikable men to me. At least Bill Gates is giving away some of his stash.

I wondered what it takes to be a billionaire. And what does it take to be successful in today's world, anyway? For Henry Kelsey, it takes clout, confidence, power to push people around, even his son.

Such are my thoughts when the door opens and a tall, well-dressed man with a briefcase strides out of the office. High-class criminal or politician; it's hard to tell. He has the billionaire's chin, though, by my study of the rich boys in the mag. Maybe that's what it takes for financial success—a certain chin, a certain look, a kind of I-don't-give-a-dog's-fart-about-anyone-else demeanour.

Right then, I vow never to join that club—not that they'd be willing to let me in.

Henry Kelsey does not look like he approves of the company his son is keeping. He doesn't really seem all that surprised to see me, but I can tell that the presence of a tall, skinny girl with short hair, tattoos and a nose piercing is throwing him off.

We go in. We sit down.

"So?" Kelsey asks his son.

"So this," Larkin says, tapping his phone lightly and handing it over to his father.

We sit in silence as Henry Kelsey watches the unedited video. His lower lip juts out as he studies the action on the screen. More than a few seconds pass.

Kelsey asks the obvious question. "Who else has seen this?"

Larkin nods at me.

"No one else?"

"Harrison took it, but he doesn't have a copy."

"So you're the only one with a copy?" The rage is building.

"I'm the only one," Larkin says.

Henry Kelsey takes the phone and heaves it with all his might at the wall. When it bounces off, he walks over and stomps on it with his shiny black shoes. It is more the dance of a madman than the handiwork of a lawyer.

When he is done stamping on it, he says simply, "That's it, then. Case closed. No one else will ever see this."

Robin begins to stand and starts to say something. Maybe it's her student-advocate role kicking in, or maybe she has her trigger finger on the bear spray. But Larkin puts a hand out to stop her.

The silence roars like a lion. I am thinking of how Kelsey had so perfectly, step by step, inch by inch, taken my father down with a look, a word, and a well-practised means of showing who was the alpha male. I stare at the smashed phone and then look at Larkin, expecting him to react.

But all he does is stand up. "Let's go," he tells Robin and me. "I'm sorry you had to see that."

Robin is bursting to shout at him. I can feel it. I am think-ing that this had all been a mistake, that I had miscalculated and have now lost my one good shot at setting the record straight. Me and my father, both, taken down without even fighting back.

We file out of the office and down the lengthy hallway to the stairs.

When we get in the car, Larkin pulls out another phone from his pocket—an expensive one this time, not at all like the burner. "I lied to him. I do have another copy," he says. "I'm the only one who has seen it other than Harrison and you. And now him, of course."

And he hands me the phone. "I say we have no choice."

He studies my face for a second. I think it's the first time Larkin and I have ever really made eye contact. He has green eyes. Who would have guessed? I knew for a fact that only two percent of the world's population has green eyes.

"JFC, you are such a goof," he says when he realizes I have second thoughts, that maybe I will not follow through and release it to the internet hordes. But there is also a hint of a smile.

He turns and holds out the phone to Robin. "You want to do the honours?"

Robin knows my side of the story, of course, but has never seen the whole video. Larkin flicks it on and she holds the phone and watches.

She studies it intently and silently and then looks up.

"You should probably post it in some anonymous way so it can't be traced back to you," Larkin tells her.

But Robin has broken into a gorgeous smile like I'd never

seen before. "No way," she says. "Yeah, I'll gladly do the honours and I want everyone to know where it's coming from."

Chapter Twenty-Six

So now I am thinking that there is light at the end of my tunnel. A way out. A way forward.

But I don't want Robin getting some new kind of bullshit problems by putting herself front and centre in this. And it might still go sour for me. I may regret his hasty decision and it will all just get worse. Here are two people trying to sort this out for me but I have a gut feeling that the stars aren't lining up.

"Don't do anything yet, Robin," I insist.

She already has the phone in her hand and is about to post the video. So far, the only person really hurting here is me. Well, me and my family. This starts me thinking about my father, who Kelsey had outgunned so easily. I like that my dad had shown his stronger side, even if he was shot down in the end. But maybe it wasn't the end.

"Larkin, you okay if I get my father into this?"

"I thought he ran for the hills years ago. Everybody knew. You never got much pity, did ya? Me, my mother ran for it once she realized the truth about the goon she'd married. I worked it, the pity thing. You'd be surprised at the mileage a guy can get out of such a thing. Especially with girls."

"Nothing much surprises me," I say. "But your old man

did a kind of shakedown thing on my father when we went there. I want to give him another shot."

"You sure? My dad loves it when he beats someone down and they come back for seconds."

"I'd like to get him back in the game."

"Sure," Larkin says. "Then let the drama unfold."

Well, the drama had already been steadily unfolding.

I am now following my gut, and thinking about stuff that Mr. Jackson had said. *Retreat first and advance later when you see advantage.* Hasn't the tide turned?

"Let me just post the damn thing," Robin says. She is antsy, anxious to get revenge. But revenge isn't what I am after, now that Larkin had come to me.

What the hell is it I want, anyway?

I want it all to work out. For everyone.

"Hand me the phone," I say.

She holds it to her chest and gives me a dirty look.

"I'm not going to erase anything. I want to call my father."

"Hand him the damn phone, Skeletor," Larkin says. The bulldozer is still operational in the Land of Larkin, but we'll have to work on that later.

I call my father, ask him first how his day is going.

"I got the job," he says. "I hate it."

"Can you meet us?"

"Why?"

I explain.

"Where shall I meet you?" he asks.

Larkin seems a little nervous now. Is *he* thinking this is some kind of trap?

Robin says, "Tell him to meet us at the Recovery Room.

The Rev can mediate, if it gets ugly."

I think, *what the heck?*, and ask my father if he can meet us there.

He says, "To hell with the damn job. I'll be right there."

We arrive there first. When we walk in, Reverend Kevin is sitting in a corner, playing his Fender Stratocaster through a little street gig amp, trying to get the riff right to an old Jimi Hendrix song, I think.

He stops playing and walks toward us. The only other person in there is Judge Shaky and he seems to be napping over top of a computer keyboard where he'd been playing chess with someone online. He seems incredibly peaceful and it makes me think, *When I get old, I'm going to do a lot of napping*.

Rev Kev scowls as soon as he is near us. "I smell cigarettes," he says, and he holds out his hand.

Robin gives him a look of sheer guilt.

"Hand 'em over."

She hands over the crumpled pack.

"Pills," he says, not asking.

She reaches in her pocket and pulls out a vial of prescription drugs of some sort.

"Weed?"

From her other pocket she extracts three rolled joints and hands them over.

"There," he says. "Don't you feel better now?"

"No," she says scornfully, but doesn't protest further.

The Rev never really asks anyone why they are there. This is his way. Everyone has their reason for being there. Everyone is accepted.

But he isn't so sure about Larkin. He gives him the once-over and must have immediately recognized him from the famous video clip.

Larkin takes the skepticism seriously. His green eyes dart away and scan the room as if he were looking for an escape route. "I'm just going to go over there and get a cup of coffee," he says, not having been asked if he wanted it.

When he has walked towards the big coffee urn, I explain to the Rev what this was about. I say my father is on his way.

The judge coughs loudly all of a sudden, wakes up and stares at the computer screen. "Holy Mother of God. I lost to that damn Russian again." He coughs some more and stands up.

There is some typical Kevin small talk. Robin toys nervously with the phone and I give her a look, insisting she do nothing yet.

More small talk, a small lecture from the judge about Russian chess tactics that North Americans fall for and, not long after his tirade is over, my father arrives. He seems a bit flustered. I don't think he fully understands what this is all about.

The Rev is his usual mellow self and tries to put him at ease by thanking him for the donation.

The wakened judge watches them intently and then blurts out, "I get a sense of extreme urgency here. What is this about?"

"Robin, show him the full-length video," I say.

She sets the phone on the table for everyone to see. Everyone but Larkin, who sits on a plastic chair by the coffee urn, sipping from a paper cup.

I don't look. Instead, I relive the scene in my head just from the sounds of Brady being slammed into the wall and then the unforgettable thump of his skull hitting the floor. I suddenly realize it was that sound—not seeing it, but hearing it—that had tripped some primitive thing in me and made me do what I did.

When the full clip is over, my dad looks at me. "It is just as you said." Not surprise, just confirmation. "Has Larkin's father seen this?"

I nod.

Reverend Kevin looks over at Larkin accusingly, but it is the judge who speaks next.

"Forget Mr. Kelsey," he says. "John Francis told me he's scheduled to go before Judge Julia Sheehan, right?"

"Right," my father says. "Go over Kelsey's head. Take this to Julia. Have the case thrown out."

Larkin must have been listening. "You do that," he says, addressing my father for the first time, "and he'll find a way to get back at you. Save yourself the pain."

But my dad has already picked up the cell phone and is putting it in his pocket. He looks at Judge Shaky.

"I'll give her a call and tell her you're coming," the judge says. "I taught her in law school. She'll be glad to see you."

Before I could say I wanted to go with him, my father is gone. But not before I catch the look of determination in his face. It is a good look. "Stay here until I get back," he tells me.

Judge Shaky clears his throat, spits something enthusiastically into a handkerchief, and turns to Robin. "Play chess?"

She nods.

"Kevin," the judge shouts, even though he doesn't need to. "Get out the real chessboard, will ya?"

Chapter Twenty-Seven

Robin beats the judge with breathtaking speed and minimal moves, while Larkin edges around the big basement hall like a nervous rhinoceros until he finds the weight-lifting equipment in the far corner.

Robin offers to play the judge another game, but he knows he doesn't stand a chance. "I'm going back to the Russian," he says, and turns on his computer.

I decide to have a cup of Recovery Room coffee. It is black and bitter and reminds me of why I don't drink coffee.

There are several stale cinnamon buns that do the trick, though, as I sit there wondering how my dad would make out. I should be worrying about my own future, I suppose. But I'm not. Don't ask me to explain it. For all I know, my dad showing the video might make everything worse, not better. I've been learning that it's a crazy, upside-down world. But maybe I'd always known that.

Robin asks Kevin if she could have just one cigarette back that she would take outside. Instead, he walks her over to the kettle weights that I'd seen her using here before.

It is the most bizarre scene I could imagine: Larkin in one corner lifting barbells with a good twenty pounds on each end, and Robin doing her rapid lift routine with the heavy, black kettle weights.

Rev comes over to me after I've finished my cinnamon buns and says, "I'm getting a vision here. Some guy who claims to be related to British royalty just donated some money for us. Maybe we need more physical equipment. A couple of rowing machines, an elliptical, stationary bikes. Looks like the weights are a hit. We could get a whole workout gym going. What do you think?"

"Couldn't hurt," I say.

I am looking at Robin and Larkin and suddenly realize that the name Larkin sounds a lot like a bird name, too. I'm sure his parents weren't thinking about that when he was born. (I believe the name Larkin originally meant "protector" or "brave warrior"—hah.) But it sounds a lot like "lark," a small English songbird. Here is this strangest of exercising duos—Robin and the Lark.

We study this odd pair, each only half glancing at the other, but obviously in competition of some sort to see who would quit first. Rev is never one to lecture me about my weight, but as we look on he says, "What's your poison? If you had to choose something physical to get in shape, what would you like to do most?"

"I don't know. My mom and I used to watch Saturday afternoon wrestling. But most of that was acting—fake stuff. I'm not much of an actor. Then she got onto watching sumo wrestling and I like that, but I don't think it would do me any good to get any heavier than I am. She got me going on UFC, too, but said that if I ever took that up, she'd kill me. And I never know for sure if she is kidding or telling the truth."

"Okay, then. Close your eyes."

I close my eyes.

"I want you to forget about that and envision doing something else—anything physical."

Eating. I could see myself sitting at the kitchen table with several brands of takeout. Clearly it is multi-national ethnic food. I daydream sometimes about the possibility of eating items of food from each continent all in one meal. I even told my mother this once and she rolled her eyes. "Including Antarctica? What dish from Antarctica should I order for you, John Francis?" I had suggested that it would probably be fish.

But I know the Rev is trying to be helpful. I won't give him my honest but silly answer.

And then, like him, I guess you could say I have a vision. Eyes still closed, thoughts of Antarctic fish swimming in my head, I see myself climbing something that looks like a wall of ice.

"I see myself climbing," I say. "But I don't think I would be good at it."

The year before, Coach Simms had put three climbing ropes in the gym and set about teaching us to be rope climbers. Larkin could do it, of course, all the way to the roof. So could a few others. Many of the rest of us failed miserably, and I was probably the worst. I barely got a metre off the ground before collapsing. I ended up flat on the floor time after time. It got some of the guys laughing so hard that snot flew out of their noses.

Coach eventually took the ropes down after Mike Roberts fell and broke his arm. Coach was pretty pissed off that he had to take them down, but the school board insisted.

"I don't think I could afford to do a climbing wall," Rev says. "They're very cool, JFC, but we don't really have the money or the space."

"All you'd need is a rope," I say.

"You want to climb up a rope?"

"Not really. In my vision, I saw myself climbing a big magnificent wall of ice, but I don't think that will happen."

I explained about the rope we had in gym.

"I suppose we could hang it from the rafters in the back of the sanctuary upstairs. Rig up a safety harness. I'd have to explain this to the congregation, though. Would you help me with that?"

"Sure," I say, realizing that, aside from this basement, I hadn't set foot in a church of any sort since I was six.

Kev motions me over to one of the computers and we start looking at rope-climbing hardware. "Much cheaper than I thought," he says. "Looks like you could attach one or two to the big beam rafter and just hook it onto the wall come Sunday so it wouldn't be in the way. If I buy it, you'll have to use it."

Realizing that he is not bullshitting me, I try to talk him out of it. "Look, I could barely lift myself off the ground when I tried this at school. I don't think you should do this. I was just kidding."

"But you saw yourself climbing?"

"I did. A wall of ice."

"But you aren't going to find a wall of ice anywhere around here and even if you did you shouldn't climb it."

"I don't know anything about climbing, really."

"I do," Rev says with that funny twinkle in his eye. "You start slow and you inch forward. Or in this case, upward."

"I don't know," I repeat.

Both Robin and Larkin are grunting now, the way jocks do in the gym when they are really pushing themselves.

The judge curses. He'd just lost another game to the damn Russian.

A full hour passes and there is no sign of my father.

Larkin gives Robin and me a ride home. He doesn't say anything at first and has his car stereo up really loud with some kind of heavy music. Robin must have snitched a cigarette from the pack Rev had taken away and is sitting in the backseat when she lights up.

Larkin suddenly turns down the music and turns back into his old self. Without taking his eyes off the road, he leans back, grabs the lit smoke from Robin's fingers and throws it out the window. "No smoking in my fucking car," he says.

Robin glares and gives him the finger, but Larkin just keeps driving and doesn't say another word to her as he pulls in her driveway and she gets out.

Chapter Twenty-Eight

You'll forgive me if I leap ahead at this point in the story. First, I should tell you that it isn't exactly happily ever after or anything like that.

But wheels are turning and, as Isaac Newton or somebody like him probably once pointed out, a body in motion tends to stay in motion until some other force changes its direction or makes it slow down. I could get into a whole philosophical lecture about inertia, but I'll leave that to your physics teacher.

So here goes.

My father comes home and apologizes for being late. He tells my mom about me calling him and that he wanted to help.

"My asshole boss told me I couldn't leave in the middle of work," he says, looking more than a little flustered. My mom's eyebrows lift a bit over his choice of words.

"So I stayed put. Just sat there at first. But then something snapped in me. I told him to go fuck himself."

"You didn't?" she says.

"I did. And then I quit. I went right on down to our son at the Recovery Room."

I nod in confirmation of the story unfolding.

"I took the evidence to Judge Julia. She kept me waiting, of course, but finally gave me a chance to present the evidence."

"And then?" my mom asks.

"She said she would dismiss the charges," he says, raising a victorious fist into the air. "It's over."

My mom is wide-eyed and smiling now. I think she might actually break into tears. It's a rare and satisfying family moment if ever there was one.

But, of course, the whole fiasco isn't really over.

We soon learn that, not long after the charges were dropped, Mr. Kelsey went raging into the courthouse, unaware that the judge had seen the video. He barged into the judge's chambers to rant, threaten and bluster until he himself was charged with disorderly conduct and nearly disbarred. Later that same day, he was stopped for drunken driving, but eventually came up with a loophole to get himself off the hook.

This does not make home life any easier for Larkin, who comes to school more than once hiding bruises on his face and neck, and sporting at least one cut lip.

Robin, for reasons she has not ever fully explained, took custody of the video again but did not post it—anonymously or otherwise.

Even though the charges had been dropped against me, Principal Morgan asserts to my parents that he is not going to back down on my termination. I am barred from even going on the school grounds to plead my case.

But Robin is still in my corner to defend me. "You gotta see this through," she insists. "You need to have a face-to-face with Morgan. You, me, Larkin. All together."

"Sounds like more trouble," I say. "Maybe it's best to leave it alone for a while."

"It doesn't work like that. Trust me."

I know that when Robin gets an idea into her head, she has to see it through.

So there I am the next day, with Robin helping me sneak into the school and hide in Oakley's small office until Mr. Battle comes to get me, around third period.

Mr. B walks me to the office and into Dr. Morgan's inner sanctum, where Robin and Larkin are already in a heated conversation with the principal.

As soon as we are in the door, Robin whips out the phone and sets it in front of Morgan.

The principal is already angered by the conspiracy that had brought us all into his office and is even hurling insults at Battle, his second in command. But I guess he can't help himself.

He watches the video, and then pushes the phone away. "Larkin, it looks like you're out as well," he finally says. "Both of you. After today, I'll make sure neither one of you sets a foot inside this school ever again."

Larkin doesn't say a word. He'd seen this coming and still had gone along with the plan.

Mr. B begins to protest, but Robin waves him away. "Dr. Morgan, you realize that there's only a handful of people who have seen this complete video. Larkin here already told me he wanted me to post it for everyone to see. I will do just that if you don't let these two students continue with their education."

194

Mantel Morgan looks like he is ready to explode. I can tell that his brain is going through the scenario: if the short version made the school look bad, what would the long version do? More big gobs of shit hitting a really large multi-speed fan.

He stares at Robin with contempt. The girl has a smirk on her face. She couldn't care less that she is really pissing off the most powerful person in the school who could make life hell for her in the days ahead.

Principal Morgan finally stands up. "Mr. Battle, can I see you outside this room?"

Battle nods and the two of them walk out into the hallway.

Robin sits stone-faced. I can't read what is going through Larkin's mind, either. Me, I feel like I am slipping into some other dimension. I haven't uttered a single word in my defence. Sometimes the best defence is no defence, right? Sometimes events unfold on their own.

No. I don't know how to describe it, really. In fact, I think my mind is empty. Whatever will be, will be.

Robin, Larkin and I sit in silence. I drift off. I don't know where they go, but I am climbing ice walls in Antarctica. There are penguins below on great islands of ice, urging me on. I can't see anything at the top, but the colour of the ice is white and blue. Very blue. The sun is out and it is bouncing spears of light off the landscape.

The principal never does return to his office. Instead, Mr. Battle walks in after five long, uneventful minutes.

"Dr. Morgan says that this is not over. He will be consulting school legal counsel. Robin, Larkin, go back to class.

John Francis, Dr. Morgan says that, under the circumstances, you can start back to classes tomorrow, after he's had a chance to inform your teachers. He asks that today you leave the school quietly. And Robin, as to the video...I don't know what to tell you."

Larkin stands up first. He doesn't look at any of us but just walks out the door.

Robin follows and says nothing but, just before she leaves, she turns and hands me the phone.

Now it is just Mr. Battle and me. He looks more his age now—an old guy who maybe wishes he'd retired from the stresses of a public high school long ago and taken it easy.

I want to thank him for his part in this. Instead, I place the phone in his hand and say, "See you tomorrow."

And with that I walk out the office door and down the familiar hallway with its smell of institutional disinfectant, sweaty high school student bodies and just the slightest whiff of cafeteria food being prepared for the frenzied school lunch hour.

My guess would be lasagne and garlic bread from the smell, probably served up with canned string beans, a bland iceberg lettuce and pale tomato salad and the optional small, waxed cardboard carton of 2% milk.

Chapter Twenty-Nine

Starting back to classes turns out to be a little messy. I have my fans and my detractors. Rude comments still float my way, some more rude than in my pre-scuffle days.

Coach Simms goes on sick leave. Our ghost of a principal is off to a lengthy conference in New York City, and in two months' time, he announces he is leaving his esteemed post to become headmaster at a posh international school in Dubai where, one can assume, the salary and prestige better match his expectations.

Mr. Battle becomes temporarily in charge of Memorial High and, before long, someone from a national educational magazine has singled him out as the "oldest working high school principal" in the country, after he passes his seventieth birthday. The head-shot on the cover of the magazine makes him look like an aging hippie god of some sort.

But no, things don't exactly "blow over", as they like to say. Larkin keeps getting into fights that Mr. Battle (his name now a bit of irony—this placator of fisticuffs) has to deal with, and with the inevitable fallout. Larkin himself seems to have become a target for the next higher level of bully boys.

The girls of a similar persuasion are equally hard on

Robin, although I could never quite understand why. Few could have fully guessed at her role in the convoluted story in which I was at the centre. Robin, however, always dishes out as good as she gets. She still walks around with that chip on her shoulder but, knowing her as well as I do, I can read an emerging confidence in her smirk, and sometimes there is even a smile.

Somebody with an indelible marker keeps scrawling filthy graffiti on my locker. I think it is Brady, but no one has been caught yet and I'll probably never know. School remains a domain in which it is a greater crime to snitch on someone doing dirty than it is to be the culprit.

I become adept at removing the comments with rubbing alcohol, toothpaste (my personal favourite), a product called Barkeeper's Friend or WD-40. I even post a now-famous three-minute YouTube video advising others how to solve their unwanted graffiti problems.

Rev Kev follows through and uses some of his new-found money to put up that climbing rope inside his church—bolted into a giant beam in the ceiling that the construction guys said was perfect for the job. And, right, you think that I'm gonna tell you I can make it all the way to the rafters. But I can't. In the kingdom of cheese sandwiches there are no heroes, remember? We all have to muddle along.

But to be honest, I like muddling.

But there is this. Rev Kev decides to change the name of the Recovery Room to just the Rec Room. It is partly a PR move to placate the neighbours, who complained about having a bunch of drug addicts and alcoholics hanging around outside.

The judge and the other regulars still use the place as a home away from home for free coffee and no-budget, low-key counselling that only the Reverend can supply. But the expanded weight collection and exercise machines bring in others—including a number of my comrades from school. Larkin and Robin are regulars, but so are a bunch of other kids who would never have otherwise set foot in there.

One of Kelsey's junior lawyers files a complaint against the church, stating that mixing teens with recovering addicts of any stripe is a horse's ass of an idea, but the Rec Room survives, and even prospers, with its own new, positive notoriety as the next-generation community centre model.

My home life is less than perfect, but it is much better than it was before all this drama. My father never went back to his job at H&R Block. He was on a natural high from boondoggling Kelsey, but that wore off and he went into a slump. The downside of the bipolar thing kicked in and he ended up on some meds that keep him level, but he regrets that they rob him of those really good days that bipolar people love to hang onto.

My mom lost her job, too, when she mouthed off at a regular customer who gave her a hard time about a batch of lousy hair care products.

However, in the one door closing and another door opening department, my father, despite his moral victory over the heinous hound Mr. Kelsey, couldn't quite bring himself to do another interview for a job that was beneath his ability. So he decided to "hang out his own shingle", which is an old, farm-town lawyer term for opening up his own office.

And he did it right out of the house. He soon got his license for family law practice and can even dabble in criminal law if the right criminal comes his way. He advertises in the town weekly for divorces, wills and anyone charged with misdemeanours or DUIs, and found that he had enough clients that he had to move the business out of the downstairs office and into the converted garage.

My mother acts as his office assistant, although she mostly runs the business while my father does the legal legwork.

No, Henry Kelsey does not come to my father for his own sequential, alcohol-related driving infractions, but Dad does send many of his DUI clients to the Rec Room for gentle Kev the Rev treatment and some potential physical exercise.

My mom and dad still fight a fair bit, but usually after business hours, and even that has died down after the first couple of months, for reasons that I'm not sure I understand. Maybe it has something to do with an improvement in their sex life after my father found a less intrusive drug to regulate his mood swings.

But a son can only guess at such things without wanting to delve too deep into them.

I should report that, as things were improving, our neighbour, the ever intuitively philosophical Mr. Jackson, kept giving us across-the-lawn speeches about "the power of ritual." We kept trying to think about something that might heal old woes and wounds, and eventually my mother brings out the bat.

"I say we bury it in the backyard," she tells my father, after he had endured a particularly taxing day of advising drunk drivers and divorce clients. They were sipping glasses of prosecco at the time, a bubbly, bottled concoction that my father had introduced into their lives, and a goodly step up from my mother's cheap, stale, and well-past-the-shelf-life red wine.

I am invited to the burial, of course, and drink a sugarless, no-name beverage that has its own bubbly texture. I help dig the oblong hole and think it a waste of a good sports instrument, but agree with Mr. J that ritual has its place—especially for spouses trying to move on to the next level of their relationship.

Thus, one Louisville Slugger was put to rest and, perhaps someday in the far-distant future, someone will dig up our back yard and find what is left of it and wonder, why would anyone bury a bat? We did not video it for posterity.

Well, Larkin and Harrison get into a tangle one day at school. I'd seen that coming from a mile off. I break it up, but take a good knock to the jaw from Harrison as Larkin relented while his opponent did not. The event does not find its way to the main office, sparing Mr. Battle and all of us further complications. But nobody shakes hands.

Larkin also gets into a wang-do at the Rec Room with Tommy, my former neighbour from my brief time in incarceration. Tommy is a bit of a yahoo who can get the goat of most anyone, so some of the other recovering coke fiends who were trying to use the stationary bike and the BowFlex have to break them up.

It proves to be nothing in the end, but it reveals that Larkin still has a long way to go to achieve sainthood, or anything remotely close, in this life.

Nonetheless, both Larkin and Robin are looking more fit than ever. Robin started eating more protein as she eased off on a starvation diet intended to help save the planet. Larkin probably didn't change his diet but just spends more time with Robin, lifting weights and doing other exercises. The two of them work out a lot together and they can often be seen walking down the hall together at school, much to the consternation of anyone nosy enough to want to offer up an opinion.

The Legend of the Robin and the Lark even seems to have overshadowed whatever story there was about me and Robin. And I don't mean to say they have a romantic relationship—but I am learning there are a lot, and I do mean a *lot*, of relationships out there that defy the usual, limited categories.

Larkin's influence, however, is not always a good one on Robin. She caught a girl scrawling insults on her own locker with a Sharpie and, before I could get to it with my toothpaste and scrubber, she did some serious hair-pulling and got her own nose piercing tugged until she bled.

I'm still working on her to get back on the pacifist path. But it's going to take some time.

~

And me, the final word on me. Or at least the *me-so-far*, since obviously a lad coming up to his seventeenth birthday is a work in progress. For the most part, I keep to myself. I've read all the literature on eating disorders at the coaching of Kevin, who buys me books from the internet. And I know there are a number of labels the medical profession would pin on me. But I boil it down to this:

I like to eat.

I mean, let's get real. In the world of addictions, some like to drink, some like their drugs, some do this or that. Me, I've always liked to eat.

But.

I cut back.

A little.

I decide that Hamburger Helper isn't that helpful. The word "salad" is not profane. A Whopper makes you feel whipped. One cheese sandwich is as good as two. (No, it really isn't, but let me say it anyway.)

My mother also has paid quite a bit of attention to our family eating habits since she buried the bat. I'm not sure I can explain how that works, but there it is. If you have a so-cially-significant bat (or other sports item, like a golf club or a tennis racket) you might try burying it and see if things improve in your family.

Pancakes are out and yogourt is in. I drink those near-tasteless, no sugar, nothing-artificial fizzy drinks. I eat a lot of celery because I read that you actually use more calories chewing celery than you get from eating it. I haven't given up pizza or ice cream. Never will. But I learned to always read the small print on the product. Never expect "frozen desert" (which looks to be ice cream but isn't) to taste like real ice cream. Go for the real thing.

So, am I still overweight? Yes. But not like before. I have a little less flab and a bit more muscle thanks to the Rec Room, some weights, the elliptical, and the now-famous church rope.

Yes, the rope. "I'm learning the rope," (singular) I say when someone asks me how I'm doing. I can do five hand-over-hand upward pulls before gravity grabs me by the ankles and tugs me back down. Five will eventually get you six and six will get you seven, and so on. One day, maybe I will touch the holy rafter of the sanctuary. Maybe not, but maybe yes.

But in my mind, I am slowly, even gracefully, climbing the great, blue-white ice wall of my life.

And the penguins are cheering me on.

So I am pleasantly amazed to see the number on the digital scale drop, little by little. Not everyone notices the weight loss, of course. But a few of the girls observe the change. Lisa, in particular.

Lisa had never given me the time of day before, probably never even noticed I existed or, if she had, had written me off as an overweight oaf.

But now it is different.

She starts out with the simple observation, "I notice that you tuck your shirt into your pants now."

For a guy like me, this is quite a compliment. "Thanks for noticing, Lisa. That's very kind of you."

She gives me a sexy little half smile. "Wow. I don't think anyone has ever called me kind before. You want to walk home together?"

I guess you could call that a gold-star day. We walk home together. The sun is out. Birds are singing. Planets are probably colliding somewhere.

Before she walks up the driveway to her big, white house, she tells me, "You know, I never realized you were so funny and…um…interesting."

"Thanks. And you, well you"—and I should stop right there—"you're not at all like I thought you were." Too late, the words are already leaving my mouth.

But she doesn't take that the wrong way. "No," she says, again with that half smile, "I'm not."

The next day at school she comes up to me at my locker. "Do you want to go out for coffee after classes?"

"I don't like coffee," I say before I even realize a girl is actually asking me out on something more or less like a date.

"Then I'll buy you a hot chocolate," she says, not batting an eye.

"Wow, really?"

"Really. My treat."

I'm flabbergasted. "Yes, then. That is so kind of you."

She playfully jabs me on the shoulder. "There you go with that kind thing again. I like you saying it, though."

So we go out and I decide to drink coffee instead of hot chocolate, feeling all sophisticated. And we talk some more as she opens up and tells me more about herself.

It turns out she is as shallow as everyone has always said she is. But I decide I like her immensely anyway.

And I like the fact that a lot of people see us together, and that it confuses them. Maybe this is one of my goals in life now: doing things that confuse people. Not sophisticated things. Not bad things. Just things.

I'd say Lisa and I are good friends and will continue to be

so, even as she chooses her next male paramour—who will not be me. But she'll still probably come to me for advice.

Other girls have taken serious notice of me and Lisa, and some of them now even make small talk with me. Robin keeps telling me to watch out for them because they are not to be trusted. So I am watching out.

And then there is this.

In the spring, the new coach, Reggie Stuart, a real shiny-faced young dude fresh out of college, takes over teaching Phys Ed. He is the ambitious type and volunteers to coach the school's first-ever wrestling team to compete against other schools.

I was hard at it, working on the new me, so I tell the old me, *What the heck. Join the frigging wrestling team. Maybe you can make your mother and father proud.*

But it isn't like those Saturday-afternoon wrestling matches we used to see on TV. There are rules. Turns out, that when it comes to fighting another mortal, I like rules.

Larkin joins, too. So you can see where this is going.

He has bulked up a bit, with more muscle (other than the muscle in his head) and I have dropped an unnecessary pound or two and suddenly we are in the same weight class.

So we learn the rules—me well, him poorly. And it isn't long before the first public intramural wrestling matches pit me, JFC, against the Lark.

The whistle blows and I find myself staring into those piercing green eyes. The bruiser in him is still there, but so is something else I can't quite label.

I still see wrestling as more of a game than a serious contest, but I quickly learn the sport. Larkin, however, does not.

He is stronger than me by far, but not so adept at the moves the new coach is teaching us.

He takes quick charge of the event, but I use his strength against him to get the advantage back. We are both amateurs and it probably looks that way to anyone watching, but we trade advantage back and forth, back and forth, until we are both sweating heavily. He has my uniform half ripped off and I have his shoved up against his face as he tries to pin me.

And then I make my move.

Body against sweaty body, I begin to reverse the situation, but before I can properly pin him to win the match, we are both on our feet, arms locked, head-to-head, breathing each other's breath, sweat dripping from our foreheads and noses, grunting like a couple of warthogs.

I think I know the exact move to make that would knock his legs out from under him and give him a right good smackdown on the mat.

But I also think that Larkin knows he has the brute strength to simply let the animal in him take over so he could swat me like an unwanted fly.

But neither one of us makes our move. We are locked together, still standing, breathing hard, grunting, grinning the grin of two adversaries satisfied to keep the battle at a stalemate right up until the whistle blows.

When we back off, I wipe the perspiration from my brow, look up at the crowd and realize Robin has been capturing the whole extraordinary thing on her phone.

end

About the author

Lesley Choyce is the author of several books of literary fiction, poetry, creative nonfiction and young adult novels. He teaches Creative Writing at Dalhousie University and his books have been published in Danish, German, Spanish, French, Swedish and Slovenian. He has won The Dartmouth Book Award, The Atlantic Poetry Prize and The Ann Connor Brimer Award and has been short-listed for the Governor-General's Award.

He lives at Lawrencetown Beach, Nova Scotia, where he surfs year-round in the North Atlantic.